The Door Through Space

The Door Through Space
by Marion Zimmer Bradley

Table of Contents

Author's Note

I've always wanted to write. But not until I discovered the old pulp science-fantasy magazines, at the age of sixteen, did this general desire become a specific urge to write science-fantasy adventures.

I took a lot of detours on the way. I discovered s-f in its golden age: the age of Kuttner, C. L. Moore, Leigh Brackett, Ed Hamilton and Jack Vance. But while I was still collecting rejection slips for my early efforts, the fashion changed. Adventures on faraway worlds and strange dimensions went out of fashion, and the new look in science-fiction—emphasis on the science—came in.

So my first stories were straight science-fiction, and I'm not trying to put down that kind of story. It has its place. By and large, the kind of science-fiction which makes tomorrow's headlines as near as this morning's coffee, has enlarged popular awareness of the modern, miraculous world of science we live in. It has helped generations of young people feel at ease with a rapidly changing world.

But fashions change, old loves return, and now that Sputniks clutter up the sky with new and unfamiliar moons, the readers of science-fiction are willing to wait for tomorrow to read tomorrow's headlines. Once again, I think, there is a place, a wish, a need and hunger for the wonder and color of the world way out. The world beyond the stars. The world we won't live to see. That is why I wrote THE DOOR THROUGH SPACE.

—Marion Zimmer Bradley

Chapter One

Beyond the spaceport gates, the men of the Kharsa were hunting down a thief. I heard the shrill cries, the pad-padding of feet in strides just a little too long and loping to be human, raising echoes all down the dark and dusty streets leading up to the main square.

But the square itself lay empty in the crimson noon of Wolf. Overhead the dim red ember of Phi Coronis, Wolf's old and dying sun, gave out a pale and heatless light. The pair of Spaceforce guards at the gates, wearing the black leathers of the Terran Empire, shockers holstered at their belts, were drowsing under the arched gateway where the star-and-rocket emblem proclaimed the domain of Terra. One of them, a snub-nosed youngster only a few weeks out from Earth, cocked an inquisitive ear at the cries and scuffling feet, then jerked his head at me.

"Hey, Cargill, you can talk their lingo. What's going on out there?"

I stepped out past the gateway to listen. There was still no one to be seen in the square. It lay white and windswept, a barricade of emptiness; to one side the spaceport and the white skyscraper of the Terran Headquarters, and at the other side, the clutter of low buildings, the street-shrine, the little spaceport cafe smelling of coffee and jaco, and the dark opening mouths of streets that rambled down into the Kharsa—the old town, the native quarter. But I was alone in the square with the shrill cries—closer now, raising echoes from the enclosing walls—and the loping of many feet down one of the dirty streets.

Then I saw him running, dodging, a hail of stones flying round his head; someone or something small and cloaked and agile. Behind him the still-faceless mob howled and threw stones. I could not yet understand the cries; but they were out for blood, and I knew it.

I said briefly, "Trouble coming," just before the mob spilled out into the square. The fleeing dwarf stared about wildly for an instant, his head jerking from side to side so rapidly that it was impossible to get even a fleeting impression of his face—human or nonhuman, familiar or bizarre. Then, like a pellet loosed from its sling, he made straight for the gateway and safety.

And behind him the loping mob yelled and howled and came pouring over half the square. Just half. Then by that sudden intuition which permeates even the most crazed mob with some semblance of reason, they came to a ragged halt, heads turning from side to side.

I stepped up on the lower step of the Headquarters building, and looked them over.

Most of them were chaks, the furred man-tall nonhumans of the Kharsa, and not the better class. Their fur was unkempt, their tails naked with filth and disease. Their leather aprons hung in tatters. One or two in the crowd were humans, the dregs of the Kharsa. But the star-and-rocket emblem blazoned across the spaceport gates sobered even the wildest blood-lust somewhat; they milled and shifted uneasily in their half of the square.

For a moment I did not see where their quarry had gone. Then I saw him crouched, not four feet from me, in a patch of shadow. Simultaneously the mob saw him, huddled just beyond the gateway, and a howl of frustration and rage went ringing round the square. Someone threw a stone. It zipped over my head, narrowly missing me, and landed at the feet of the black-leathered guard. He jerked his head up and gestured with the shocker which had suddenly come unholstered.

The gesture should have been enough. On Wolf, Terran law has been written in blood and fire and exploding atoms; and the line is drawn firm and clear. The men of Spaceforce do not interfere in the old town, or in any of the native cities. But when violence steps over the threshold, passing the blazon of the star and rocket, punishment is swift and terrible. The threat should have been enough.

Instead a howl of abuse went up from the crowd.

"Terranan!"

"Son of the Ape!"

The Spaceforce guards were shoulder to shoulder behind me now. The snub-nosed kid, looking slightly pale, called out. "Get inside the gates, Cargill! If I have to shoot—"

The older man motioned him to silence. "Wait. Cargill," he called.

I nodded to show that I heard.

"You talk their lingo. Tell them to haul off! Damned if I want to shoot!"

I stepped down and walked into the open square, across the crumbled white stones, toward the ragged mob. Even with two armed Spaceforce men at my back, it made my skin crawl, but I flung up my empty hand in token of peace:

"Take your mob out of the square," I shouted in the jargon of the Kharsa. "This territory is held in compact of peace! Settle your quarrels elsewhere!"

There was a little stirring in the crowd. The shock of being addressed in their own tongue, instead of the Terran Standard which the Empire has forced on Wolf, held them silent for a minute. I had learned that long ago: that speaking in any of the languages of Wolf would give me a minute's advantage.

But only a minute. Then one of the mob yelled, "We'll go if you give'm to us! He's no right to Terran sanctuary!"

I walked over to the huddled dwarf, miserably trying to make himself smaller against the wall. I nudged him with my foot.

"Get up. Who are you?"

The hood fell away from his face as he twitched to his feet. He was trembling violently. In the shadow of the hood I saw a furred face, a quivering velvety muzzle, and great soft golden eyes which held intelligence and terror.

"What have you done? Can't you talk?"

He held out the tray which he had shielded under his cloak, an ordinary peddler's tray. "Toys. Sell toys. Children. You got'm?"

I shook my head and pushed the creature away, with only a glance at the array of delicately crafted manikins, tiny animals, prisms and crystal whirligigs. "You'd better get out of here. Scram. Down that street." I pointed.

A voice from the crowd shouted again, and it had a very ugly sound. "He is a spy of Nebran!"

"Nebran—" The dwarfish nonhuman gabbled something then doubled behind me. I saw him dodge, feint in the direction of the gates, then, as the crowd surged that way, run for the street-shrine across the square, slipping from recess to recess of the wall. A hail of stones went flying in that direction. The little toy-seller dodged into the street-shrine.

Then there was a hoarse "Ah, aaah!" of terror, and the crowd edged away, surged backward. The next minute it had begun to melt away, its entity dissolving into separate creatures, slipping into the side alleys and the dark streets that disgorged into the square. Within three minutes the square lay empty again in the pale-crimson noon.

The kid in black leather let his breath go and swore, slipping his shocker into its holster. He stared and demanded profanely, "Where'd the little fellow go?"

"Who knows?" the other shrugged. "Probably sneaked into one of the alleys. Did you see where he went, Cargill?"

I came slowly back to the gateway. To me, it had seemed that he ducked into the street-shrine and vanished into thin air, but I've lived on Wolf long enough to know you can't trust your eyes here. I said so, and the kid swore again, gulping, more upset than he wanted to admit. "Does this kind of thing happen often?"

"All the time," his companion assured him soberly, with a sidewise wink at me. I didn't return the wink.

The kid wouldn't let it drop. "Where did you learn their lingo, Mr. Cargill?"

"I've been on Wolf a long time," I said, spun on my heel and walked toward Headquarters. I tried not to hear, but their voices followed me anyhow, discreetly lowered, but not lowered enough.

"Kid, don't you know who he is? That's Cargill of the Secret Service! Six years ago he was the best man in Intelligence, before—" The voice lowered another decibel, and then there was the kid's voice asking, shaken, "But what the hell happened to his face?"

I should have been used to it by now. I'd been hearing it, more or less behind my back, for six years. Well, if my luck held, I'd never hear it again. I strode up the white steps of the skyscraper, to finish the arrangements that would take me away from Wolf forever. To the other end of the Empire, to the other end of the galaxy—anywhere, so long as I need not wear my past like a medallion around my neck, or blazoned and branded on what was left of my ruined face.

Chapter Two

The Terran Empire has set its blazon on four hundred planets circling more than three hundred suns. But no matter what the color of the sun, the number of moons overhead, or the geography of the planet, once you step inside a Headquarters building, you are on Earth. And Earth would be alien to many who called themselves Earthmen, judging by the strangeness I always felt when I stepped into that marble-and-glass world inside the skyscraper. I heard the sound of my steps ringing into thin resonance along the marble corridor, and squinted my eyes, readjusting them painfully to the cold yellowness of the lights.

The Traffic Division was efficiency made insolent, in glass and chrome and polished steel, mirrors and windows and looming electronic clerical machines. Most of one wall was taken up by a TV monitor which gave a view of the spaceport; a vast open space lighted with blue-white mercury vapor lamps, and a chained-down skyscraper of a starship, littered over with swarming ants. The process crew was getting the big ship ready for skylift tomorrow morning. I gave it a second and then a third look. I'd be on it when it lifted.

Turning away from the monitored spaceport, I watched myself stride forward in the mirrored surfaces that were everywhere; a tall man, a lean man, bleached out by years under a red sun, and deeply scarred on both cheeks and around the mouth. Even after six years behind a desk, my neat business clothes—suitable for an Earthman with a desk job—didn't fit quite right, and I still rose unconsciously on the balls of my feet, approximating the lean stooping walk of a Dry-towner from the Coronis plains.

The clerk behind the sign marked TRANSPORTATION was a little rabbit of a man with a sunlamp tan, barricaded by a small-sized spaceport of desk, and looking as if he liked being shut up there. He looked up in civil inquiry.

"Can I do something for you?"

"My name's Cargill. Have you a pass for me?"

He stared. A free pass aboard a starship is rare except for professional spacemen, which I obviously wasn't. "Let me check my records," he hedged, and punched scanning buttons on the glassy surface. Shadows came and went, and I saw myself half-reflected, a tipsy shadow in a flurry of racing colors. The pattern finally stabilized and the clerk read off names.

"Brill, Cameron ... ah, yes. Cargill, Race Andrew, Department 38, transfer transportation. Is that you?"

I admitted it and he started punching more buttons when the sound of the name made connection in whatever desk-clerks use for a brain. He stopped with his hand halfway to the button.

"Are you Race Cargill of the Secret Service, sir? The Race Cargill?"

"It's right there," I said, gesturing wearily at the projected pattern under the glassy surface.

"Why, I thought—I mean, everybody took it for granted—that is, I heard—"

"You thought Cargill had been killed a long time ago because his name never turned up in news dispatches any more?" I grinned sourly, seeing my image dissolve in blurring shadows, and feeling the long-healed scar on my mouth draw up to make the grin hideous. "I'm Cargill, all right. I've been up on Floor 38 for six years, holding down a desk any clerk could handle. You for instance."

He gaped. He was a rabbit of a man who had never stepped out of the safe familiar boundaries of the Terran Trade City. "You mean you're the man who went to Charin in disguise, and routed out The Lisse? The man who scouted the Black Ridge and Shainsa? And you've been working at a desk upstairs all these years? It's—hard to believe, sir."

My mouth twitched. It had been hard for me to believe while I was doing it. "The pass?"

"Right away, sir." He punched buttons and a printed chip of plastic extruded from a slot on the desk top. "Your fingerprint, please?" He pressed my finger into the still-soft surface of the plastic, indelibly recording the print; waited a moment for it to harden, then laid the chip in the slot of a pneumatic tube. I heard it whoosh away.

"They'll check your fingerprint against that when you board the ship. Skylift isn't till dawn, but you can go aboard as soon as the process crew finishes with her." He glanced at the monitor screen, where the swarming crew were still doing inexplicable things to the immobile spacecraft. "It will be another hour or two. Where are you going, Mr. Cargill?"

"Some planet in the Hyades Cluster. Vainwal, I think, something like that."

"What's it like there?"

"How should I know?" I'd never been there either. I only knew that Vainwal had a red sun, and that the Terran Legate could use a trained Intelligence officer. And not pin him down to a desk.

There was respect, and even envy in the little man's voice. "Could I—buy you a drink before you go aboard, Mr. Cargill?"

"Thanks, but I have a few loose ends to tie up." I didn't, but I was damned if I'd spend my last hour on Wolf under the eyes of a deskbound rabbit who preferred his adventure safely secondhand.

But after I'd left the office and the building, I almost wished I'd taken him up on it. It would be at least an hour before I could board the starship, with nothing to do but hash over old memories, better forgotten.

The sun was lower now. Phi Coronis is a dim star, a dying star, and once past the crimson zenith of noon, its light slants into a long pale-reddish twilight. Four of Wolf's five moons were clustered in a pale bouquet overhead, mingling thin violet moonlight into the crimson dusk.

The shadows were blue and purple in the empty square as I walked across the stones and stood looking down one of the side streets.

A few steps, and I was in an untidy slum which might have been on another world from the neat bright Trade City which lay west of the spaceport. The Kharsa was alive and reeking with the sounds and smells of human and half-human life. A naked child, diminutive and golden-furred, darted between two of the chinked pebble-houses, and disappeared, spilling fragile laughter like breaking glass.

A little beast, half snake and half cat, crawled across a roof, spread leathery wings, and flapped to the ground. The sour pungent reek of incense from the open street-shrine made my nostrils twitch, and a hulked form inside, not human, cast me a surly green glare as I passed.

I turned, retracing my steps. There was no danger, of course, so close to the Trade City. Even on such planets as Wolf, Terra's laws are respected within earshot of their gates. But there had been rioting here and in Charin during the last month. After the display of mob violence this afternoon, a lone Terran, unarmed, might turn up as a solitary corpse flung on the steps of the HQ building.

There had been a time when I had walked alone from Shainsa to the Polar Colony. I had known how to melt into this kind of night, shabby and inconspicuous, a worn shirtcloak hunched round my shoulders, weaponless except for the razor-sharp skean in the clasp of the cloak; walking on the balls of my feet like a Dry-towner, not looking or sounding or smelling like an Earthman.

That rabbit in the Traffic office had stirred up things I'd be wiser to forget. It had been six years; six years of slow death behind a desk, since the day when Rakhal Sensar had left me a marked man; death-warrant written on my scarred face anywhere outside the narrow confines of the Terran law on Wolf.

Rakhal Sensar—my fists clenched with the old impotent hate. If I could get my hands on him!

It had been Rakhal who first led me through the byways of the Kharsa, teaching me the jargon of a dozen tribes, the chirping call of the Ya-men, the way of the catmen of the rain-forests, the argot of thieves markets, the walk and step of the Dry-towners from Shainsa and Daillon and Ardcarran—the parched cities of dusty, salt stone which spread out in the bottoms of Wolf's vanished oceans. Rakhal was from Shainsa, human, tall as an Earthman, weathered by salt and sun, and he had worked for Terran Intelligence since we were boys. We had traveled all over our world together, and found it good.

And then, for some reason I had never known, it had come to an end. Even now I was not wholly sure why he had erupted, that day, into violence and a final explosion. Then he had disappeared, leaving me a marked man. And a lonely one: Juli had gone with him.

I strode the streets of the slum unseeing, my thoughts running a familiar channel. Juli, my kid sister, clinging around Rakhal's neck, her gray eyes hating me. I had never seen her again.

That had been six years ago. One more adventure had shown me that my usefulness to the Secret Service was over. Rakhal had vanished, but he had left me a legacy: my name, written on the sure scrolls of death anywhere outside the safe boundaries of Terran law. A marked man, I had gone back to slow stagnation behind a desk. I'd stood it as long as I could.

When it finally got too bad, Magnusson had been sympathetic. He was the Chief of Terran Intelligence on Wolf, and I was next in line for his job, but he understood when I quit. He'd arranged the transfer and the pass, and I was leaving tonight.

I was nearly back to the spaceport by now, across from the street-shrine at the edge of the square. It was here that the little toy-seller had vanished. But it was exactly like a thousand, a hundred thousand other such street-shrines on Wolf, a smudge of incense reeking and stinking before the squatting image of Nebran, the Toad God whose face and symbol are everywhere on Wolf. I stared for a moment at the ugly idol, then slowly moved away.

The lighted curtains of the spaceport cafe attracted my attention and I went inside. A few spaceport personnel in storm gear were drinking coffee at the counter, a pair of furred chaks, lounging beneath the mirrors at the far end, and a trio of Dry-towners, rangy, weathered men in crimson and blue shirt cloaks, were standing at a wall shelf, eating Terran food with aloof dignity.

In my business clothes I felt more conspicuous than the chaks. What place had a civilian here, between the uniforms of the spacemen and the colorful brilliance of the Dry-towners?

A snub-nosed girl with alabaster hair came to take my order. I asked for jaco and bunlets, and carried the food to a wall shelf near the Dry-towners. Their dialect fell soft and familiar on my ears. One of them, without altering the expression on his face or the easy tone of his voice, began to make elaborate comments on my entrance, my appearance, my ancestry and probably personal habits, all defined in the colorfully obscene dialect of Shainsa.

That had happened before. The Wolfan sense of humor is only half-human. The finest joke is to criticize and insult a stranger, preferably an Earthman, to his very face, in an unknown language, perfectly deadpan. In my civilian clothes I was obviously fair game.

A look or gesture of resentment would have lost face and dignity—what the Dry-towners call their kihar—permanently. I leaned over and remarked in their own dialect that I would, at some future and unspecified time, appreciate the opportunity to return their compliments.

By rights they should have laughed, made some barbed remark about my command of language and crossed their hands in symbol of a jest decently reversed on themselves. Then we would have bought each other a drink, and that would be that.

But it didn't happen that way. Not this time. The tallest of the three whirled, upsetting his drink in the process. I heard its thin shatter through the squeal of the alabaster-haired girl, as a chair crashed over. They faced me three abreast, and one of them fumbled in the clasp of his shirtcloak.

I edged backward, my own hand racing up for a skean I hadn't carried in six years, and fronted them squarely, hoping I could face down the prospect of a roughhouse. They wouldn't kill me, this close to the HQ, but at least I was in for an unpleasant mauling. I couldn't handle three men; and if nerves were this taut in the Kharsa, I might get knifed. Quite by accident, of course.

The chaks moaned and gibbered. The Dry-towners glared at me and I tensed for the moment when their steady stare would explode into violence.

Then I became aware that they were gazing, not at me, but at something or someone behind me. The skeans snicked back into the clasps of their cloaks.

Then they broke rank, turned and ran. They ran, blundering into stools, leaving havoc of upset benches and broken crockery in their wake. One man barged into the counter, swore and ran on, limping. I let my breath go. Something had put the fear of God into those brutes, and it wasn't my own ugly mug. I turned and saw the girl.

She was slight, with waving hair like spun black glass, circled with faint tracery of stars. A black glass belt bound her narrow waist like clasped hands, and her robe, stark white, bore an ugly embroidery across the breasts, the flat sprawl of a conventionalized Toad God, Nebran. Her features were delicate, chiseled, pale; a Dry-town face, all human, all woman, but set in an alien and unearthly repose. The great eyes gleamed red. They were fixed, almost unseeing, but the crimson lips were curved with inhuman malice.

She stood motionless, looking at me as if wondering why I had not run with the others. In half a second, the smile flickered off and was replaced by a startled look of—recognition?

Whoever and whatever she was, she had saved me a mauling. I started to phrase formal thanks, then broke off in astonishment. The cafe had emptied and we were entirely alone. Even the chaks had leaped through an open window—I saw the whisk of a disappearing tail.

We stood frozen, looking at one another while the Toad God sprawled across her breasts rose and fell for half a dozen breaths.

Then I took one step forward, and she took one step backward, at the same instant. In one swift movement she was outside in the dark street. It took me only an instant to get into the street after her, but as I stepped across the door there was a little stirring in the air, like the rising of heat waves across the salt flats at noon. Then the street-shrine was empty, and nowhere was there any sign of the girl. She had vanished. She simply was not there.

I gaped at the empty shrine. She had stepped inside and vanished, like a wraith of smoke, like—

—Like the little toy-seller they had hunted out of the Kharsa.

There were eyes in the street again and, becoming aware of where I was, I moved away. The shrines of Nebran are on every corner of Wolf, but this is one instance when familiarity does not breed contempt. The street was dark and seemed empty, but it was packed with all the little noises of living. I was not unobserved. And meddling with a street-shrine would be just as dangerous as the skeans of my three loud-mouthed Dry-town roughnecks.

I turned and crossed the square for the last time, turning toward the loom of the spaceship, filing the girl away as just another riddle of Wolf I'd never solve.

How wrong I was!

Chapter Three

From the spaceport gates, exchanging brief greetings with the guards, I took a last look at the Kharsa. For a minute I toyed with the notion of just disappearing down one of those streets. It's not hard to disappear on Wolf, if you know how. And I knew, or had known once. Loyalty to Terra? What had Terra given me except a taste of color and adventure, out there in the Dry-towns, and then taken it away again?

If an Earthman is very lucky and very careful, he lasts about ten years in Intelligence. I had had two years more than my share. I still knew enough to leave my Terran identity behind like a worn-out jacket. I could seek out Rakhal, settle our blood-feud, see Juli again....

How could I see Juli again? As her husband's murderer? No other way. Blood-feud on Wolf is a terrible and elaborate ritual of the code duello. And once I stepped outside the borders of Terran law, sooner or later Rakhal and I would meet. And one of us would die.

I looked back, just once, at the dark rambling streets away from the square. Then I turned toward the blue-white lights that hurt my eyes, and the starship that loomed, huge and hateful, before me.

A steward in white took my fingerprint and led me to a coffin-sized chamber. He brought me coffee and sandwiches—I hadn't, after all, eaten in the spaceport cafe—then got me into the skyhook and strapped me, deftly and firmly, into the acceleration cushions, tugging at the Garensen belts until I ached all over. A long needle went into my arm—the narcotic that would keep me safely drowsy all through the terrible tug of interstellar acceleration.

Doors clanged, buzzers vibrated lower down in the ship, men tramped the corridors calling to one another in the language of the spaceports. I understood one word in four. I shut my eyes, not caring. At the end of the trip there would be another star, another world, another language. Another life.

I had spent all my adult life on Wolf. Juli had been a child under the red star. But it was a pair of wide crimson eyes and black hair combed into ringlets like spun black glass that went down with me into the bottomless pit of sleep....

Someone was shaking me.

"Ah, come on, Cargill. Wake up, man. Shake your boots!"

My mouth, foul-tasting and stiff, fumbled at the shapes of words. "Wha' happened? Wha' y' want?" My eyes throbbed. When I got them open I saw two men in black leathers bending over me. We were still inside gravity.

"Get out of the skyhook. You're coming with us."

"Wha'—" Even through the layers of the sedative, that got to me. Only a criminal, under interstellar law, can be removed from a passage-paid starship once he has formally checked in on board. I was legally, at this moment, on my "planet of destination."

"I haven't been charged—"

"Did I say you had?" snapped one man.

"Shut up, he's doped," the other said hurriedly. "Look," he continued, pronouncing every word loudly and distinctly, "get up now, and come with us. The co-ordinator will hold up blastoff if we don't get off in three minutes, and Operations will scream. Come on, please."

Then I was stumbling along the lighted, empty corridor, swaying between the two men, foggily realizing the crew must think me a fugitive caught trying to leave the planet.

The locks dilated. A uniformed spaceman watched us, fussily regarding a chronometer. He fretted. "The dispatcher's office—"

"We're doing the best we can," the Spaceforce man said. "Can you walk, Cargill?"

I could, though my feet were a little shaky on the ladders. The violet moonlight had deepened to mauve, and gusty winds spun tendrils of grit across my face. The Spaceforce men shepherded me, one on either side, to the gateway.

"What the hell is all this? Is something wrong with my pass?"

The guard shook his head. "How would I know? Magnusson put out the order, take it up with him."

"Believe me," I muttered, "I will."

They looked at each other. "Hell," said one, "he's not under arrest, we don't have to haul him around like a convict. Can you walk all right now, Cargill? You know where the Secret Service office is, don't you? Floor 38. The Chief wants you, and make it fast."

I knew it made no sense to ask questions, they obviously knew no more than I did. I asked anyhow.

"Are they holding the ship for me? I'm supposed to be leaving on it."

"Not that one," the guard answered, jerking his head toward the spaceport. I looked back just in time to see the dust-dimmed ship leap upward, briefly whitened in the field searchlights, and vanish into the surging clouds above.

My head was clearing fast, and anger speeded up the process. The HQ building was empty in the chill silence of just before dawn. I had to rout out a dozing elevator operator, and as the lift swooped upward my anger rose with it. I wasn't working for Magnusson any more. What right had he, or anybody, to grab me off an outbound starship like a criminal? By the time I barged into his office, I was spoiling for a fight.

The Secret Service office was full of grayish-pink morning and yellow lights left on from the night before. Magnusson, at his desk, looked as if he'd slept in his rumpled uniform. He was a big bull of a man, and his littered desk looked, as always, like the track of a typhoon in the salt flats.

The clutter was weighted down, here and there, with solidopic cubes of the five Magnusson youngsters, and as usual, Magnusson was fiddling with one of the cubes. He said, not looking up, "Sorry to pull this at the last minute, Race. There was just time to put out a pull order and get you off the ship, but no time to explain."

I glared at him. "Seems I can't even get off the planet without trouble! You raised hell all the time I was here, but when I try to leave—what is this, anyhow? I'm sick of being shoved around!"

Magnusson made a conciliating gesture. "Wait until you hear—" he began, and broke off, looking at someone who was sitting in the chair in front of his desk, somebody whose back was turned to me. Then the person twisted and I stopped cold, blinking and wondering if this were a hallucination and I'd wake up in the starship's skyhook, far out in space.

Then the woman cried, "Race, Race! Don't you know me?"

I took one dazed step and another. Then she flew across the space between us, her thin arms tangling around my neck, and I caught her up, still disbelieving.

"Juli!"

"Oh, Race, I thought I'd die when Mack told me you were leaving tonight. It's been the only thing that's kept me alive, knowing—knowing I'd see you." She sobbed and laughed, her face buried in my shoulder.

I let her cry for a minute, then held my sister at arm's length. For a moment I had forgotten the six years that lay between us. Now I saw them, all of them, printed plain on her face. Juli had been a pretty girl. Six years had fined her face into beauty, but there was tension in the set of her shoulders, and her gray eyes had looked on horrors.

She looked tiny and thin and unbearably frail under the scanty folds of her fur robe, a Dry-town woman's robe. Her wrists were manacled, the jeweled tight bracelets fastened together by the links of a long fine chain of silvered gilt that clashed a little, thinly, as her hands fell to her sides.

"What's wrong, Juli? Where's Rakhal?"

She shivered and now I could see that she was in a state of shock.

"Gone. He's gone, that's all I know. And—oh, Race, Race, he took Rindy with him!"

From the tone of her voice I had thought she was sobbing. Now I realized that her eyes were dry; she was long past tears. Gently I unclasped her clenched fingers and put her back in the chair. She sat like a doll, her hands falling to her sides with a thin clash of chains. When I picked them up and laid them in her lap she let them lie there motionless. I stood over her and demanded, "Who's Rindy?" She didn't move.

"My daughter, Race. Our little girl."

Magnusson broke in, his voice harsh. "Well, Cargill, should I have let you leave?"

"Don't be a damn fool!"

"I was afraid you'd tell the poor kid she had to live with her own mistakes," growled Magnusson. "You're capable of it."

For the first time Juli showed a sign of animation. "I was afraid to come to you, Mack. You never wanted me to marry Rakhal, either."

"Water under the bridge," Magnusson grunted. "And I've got lads of my own, Miss Cargill—Mrs.—" he stopped in distress, vaguely remembering that in the Dry-towns an improper form of address can be a deadly insult.

But she guessed his predicament.

"You used to call me Juli, Mack. It will do now."

"You've changed," he said quietly. "Juli, then. Tell Race what you told me. All of it."

She turned to me. "I shouldn't have come for myself—"

I knew that. Juli was proud, and she had always had the courage to live with her own mistakes. When I first saw her, I knew this wouldn't be anything so simple as the complaint of an abused wife or even an abandoned or deserted mother. I took a chair, watching her and listening.

She began. "You made a mistake when you turned Rakhal out of the Service, Mack. In his way he was the most loyal man you had on Wolf."

Magnusson had evidently not expected her to take this tack. He scowled and looked disconcerted, shifting uneasily in his big chair, but when Juli did not continue, obviously awaiting his answer, he said, "Juli, he left me no choice. I never knew how his mind worked. That final deal he engineered—have you any idea how much that cost the Service? And have you taken a good look at your brother's face, Juli girl?"

Juli raised her eyes slowly, and I saw her flinch. I knew how she felt. For three years I had kept my mirror covered, growing an untidy straggle of beard because it hid the scars and saved me the ordeal of facing myself to shave.

Juli whispered, "Rakhal's is just as bad. Worse."

"That's some satisfaction," I said, and Mack stared at us, baffled. "Even now I don't know what it was all about."

"And you never will," I said for the hundredth time. "We've been over this before. Nobody could understand it unless he'd lived in the Dry-towns. Let's not talk about it. You talk, Juli. What brought you here like this? What about the kid?"

"There's no way I can tell you the end without telling you the beginning," she said reasonably. "At first Rakhal worked as a trader in Shainsa."

I wasn't surprised. The Dry-towns were the core of Terran trade on Wolf, and it was through their cooperation that Terra existed here peaceably, on a world only half human, or less.

The men of the Dry-towns existed strangely poised between two worlds. They had made dealings with the first Terran ships, and thus gave entrance to the wedge of the Terran Empire. And yet they stood proud and apart. They alone had never yielded to the Terranizing which overtakes all Empire planets sooner or later.

There were no Trade Cities in the Dry-towns; an Earthman who went there unprotected faced a thousand deaths, each one worse than the last. There were those who said that the men of Shainsa and Daillon and Ardcarran had sold the rest of Wolf to the Terrans, to keep the Terrans from their own door.

Even Rakhal, who had worked with Terra since boyhood, had finally come to a point of decision and gone his own way. And it was not Terra's way.

That was what Juli was saying now.

"He didn't like what Terra was doing on Wolf. I'm not so sure I like it myself—"

Magnusson interrupted her again. "Do you know what Wolf was like when we came here? Have you seen the Slave Colony, the Idiot's Village? Your own brother went to Shainsa and routed out The Lisse."

"And Rakhal helped him!" Juli reminded him. "Even after he left you, he tried to keep out of things. He could have told them a good deal that would hurt you, after ten years in Intelligence, you know."

I knew. It was, although I wasn't going to tell Juli this, one reason why, at the end—during that terrible explosion of violence which no normal Terran mind could comprehend—I had done my best to kill him. We had both known that after this, the planet would not hold the two of us. We could both go on living only by dividing it unevenly. I had been given the slow death of the Terran Zone. And he had all the rest.

"But he never told them anything! I tell you, he was one of the most loyal—"

Mack grunted, "Yeah, he's an angel. Go ahead."

She didn't, not immediately. Instead she asked what sounded like an irrelevant question. "Is it true what he told me? That the Empire has a standing offer of a reward for a working model of a matter transmitter?"

"That offer's been standing for three hundred years, Terran reckoning. One million credits cash. Don't tell me he was figuring to invent one?"

"I don't think so. But I think he heard rumors about one. He said with that kind of money he could bargain the Terrans right out of Shainsa. That was where it started. He began coming and going at odd times, but he never said any more about it. He wouldn't talk to me at all."

"When was all this?"

"About four months ago."

"In other words, just about the time of the riots in Charin."

She nodded. "Yes. He was away in Charin when the Ghost Wind blew, and he came back with knife cuts in his thigh. I asked if he had been mixed-up in the anti-Terran rioting, but he wouldn't tell me. Race, I don't know anything about politics. I don't really care. But just about that time, the Great House in Shainsa changed hands. I'm sure Rakhal had something to do with that.

"And then—" Juli twisted her chained hands together in her lap—"he tried to mix Rindy up in it. It was crazy, awful! He'd brought her some sort of nonhuman toy from one of the lowland towns, Charin I think. It was a weird thing, scared me. But he'd sit Rindy down in the sunlight and have her look into it, and Rindy would gabble all sorts of nonsense about little men and birds and a toymaker."

The chains about Juli's wrists clashed as she twisted her hands together. I stared somberly at the fetters. The chain, which was long, did not really hamper her movements much. Such chains were symbolic ornaments, and most Dry-town women went all their lives with fettered hands. But even after the years I'd spent in the Dry-towns, the sight still brought an uneasiness to my throat, a vague discomfort.

"We had a terrible fight over that," Juli went on. "I was afraid, afraid of what it was doing to Rindy. I threw it out, and Rindy woke up and screamed—" Juli checked herself and caught at vanishing self-control.

"But you don't want to hear about that. It was then I threatened to leave him and take Rindy. The next day—" Suddenly the hysteria Juli had been forcing back broke free, and she rocked back and forth in her chair, shaken and strangled with sobs. "He took Rindy! Oh, Race, he's crazy, crazy. I think he hates Rindy, he—he, Race, he smashed her toys. He took every toy the child had and broke them one by one, smashed them into powder, every toy the child had—"

"Juli, please, please," Magnusson pleaded, shaken. "If we're dealing with a maniac—"

"I don't dare think he'd harm her! He warned me not to come here, or I'd never see her again, but if it meant war against Terra I had to come. But Mack, please, don't do anything against him, please, please. He's got my baby, he's got my little girl...." Her voice failed and she buried her face in her hands.

Mack picked up the solidopic cube of his five-year-old son, and turned it between his pudgy fingers, saying unhappily, "Juli, we'll take every precaution. But can't you see, we've got to get him? If there's a question of a matter transmitter, or anything like that, in the hands of Terra's enemies—"

I could see that, too, but Juli's agonized face came between me and the picture of disaster. I clenched my fist around the chair arm, not surprised to see the fragile plastic buckle, crack and split under my grip. If it had been Rakhal's neck....

"Mack, let me handle this. Juli, shall I find Rindy for you?"

A hope was born in her ravaged face, and died, while I looked. "Race, he'd kill you. Or have you killed."

"He'd try," I admitted. The moment Rakhal knew I was outside the Terran zone, I'd walk with death. I had accepted the code during my years in Shainsa. But now I was an Earthman and felt only contempt.

"Can't you see? Once he knows I'm at large, that very code of his will force him to abandon any intrigue, whatever you call it, conspiracy, and come after me first. That way we do two things: we get him out of hiding, and we get him out of the conspiracy, if there is one."

I looked at the shaking Juli and something snapped. I stooped and lifted her, not gently, my hands biting her shoulders. "And I won't kill him, do you hear? He may wish I had; by the time I get through with him—I'll beat the living hell out of him; I'll cram my fists down his throat. But I'll settle it with him like an Earthman. I won't kill him. Hear me, Juli? Because that's the worst thing I could do to him—catch him and let him live afterward!"

Magnusson stepped toward me and pried my crushing hands off her arms. Juli rubbed the bruises mechanically, not knowing she was doing it. Mack said, "You can't do it, Cargill. You wouldn't get as far as Daillon. You haven't been out of the zone in six years. Besides—"

His eyes rested full on my face. "I hate to say this, Race, but damn it, man, go and take a good look at yourself in a mirror. Do you think I'd ever have pulled you off the Secret Service otherwise? How in hell can you disguise yourself now?"

"There are plenty of scarred men in the Dry-towns," I said. "Rakhal will remember my scars, but I don't think anyone else would look twice."

Magnusson walked to the window. His huge form bulked against the light, perceptibly darkening the office. He looked over the faraway panorama, the neat bright Trade City below and the vast wilderness lying outside. I could almost hear the wheels grinding in his head. Finally he swung around.

"Race, I've heard these rumors before. But you're the only man I could have sent to track them down, and I wouldn't send you out in cold blood to be killed. I won't now. Spaceforce will pick him up."

I heard the harsh inward gasp of Juli's breath and said, "Damn it, no. The first move you make—" I couldn't finish. Rindy was in his hands, and when I knew Rakhal, he hadn't been given to making idle threats. We all three knew what Rakhal might do at the first hint of the long arm of Terran law reaching out for him.

I said, "For God's sake let's keep Spaceforce out of it. Let it look like a personal matter between Rakhal and me, and let us settle it on those terms. Remember he's got the kid."

Magnusson sighed. Again he picked up one of the cubes and stared into the clear plastic, where the three-dimensional image of a nine-year-old girl looked out at him, smiling and innocent. His face was transparent as the plastic cube. Mack acts tough, but he has five kids and he is as soft as a dish of pudding where a kid is concerned.

"I know. Another thing, too. If we send out Spaceforce, after all the riots—how many Terrans are on this planet? A few thousand, no more. What chance would we have, if it turned into a full-scale rebellion? None at all, unless we wanted to order a massacre. Sure, we have bombs and dis-guns and all that.

"But would we dare to use them? And where would we be after that? We're here to keep the pot from boiling over, to keep out of planetary incidents, not push them along to a point where bluff won't work. That's why we've got to pick up Rakhal before this gets out of hand."

I said, "Give me a month. Then you can move in, if you have to. Rakhal can't do much against Terra in that time. And I might be able to keep Rindy out of it."

Magnusson stared at me, hard-eyed. "If you do this against my advice, I won't be able to step in and pull you out of a jam later on, you know. And God help you if you start up the machines and can't stop them."

I knew that. A month wasn't much. Wolf is forty thousand miles of diameter, at least half unexplored; mountain and forest swarming with nonhuman and semi-human cities where Terrans had never been.

Finding Rakhal, or any one man, would be like picking out one star in the Andromeda nebula. Not impossible. Not quite impossible.

Mack's eyes wandered again to his child's face, deep in the transparent cube. He turned it in his hands. "Okay, Cargill," he said slowly, "so we're all crazy. I'll be crazy too. Try it your way."

Chapter Four

By sunset I was ready to leave. I hadn't had any loose ends to tie up in the Trade City, since I'd already disposed of most of my gear before boarding the starship. I'd never been in better circumstances to take off for parts unknown.

Mack, still disapproving, had opened the files to me, and I'd spent most of the day in the back rooms of Floor 38, searching Intelligence files to refresh my memory, scanning the pages of my own old reports sent years ago from Shainsa and Daillon. He had sent out one of the nonhumans who worked for us, to buy or acquire somewhere in the Old Town a Dry-towner's outfit and the other things I would wear and carry.

I would have liked to go myself. I felt that I needed the practice. I was only now beginning to realize how much I might have forgotten in the years behind a desk. But until I was ready to make my presence known, no one must know that Race Cargill had not left Wolf on the starship.

Above all, I must not be seen in the Kharsa until I went there in the Dry-town disguise which had become, years ago, a deep second nature, almost an alternate personality.

About sunset I walked through the clean little streets of the Terran Trade City toward the Magnusson home where Juli was waiting for me.

Most of the men who go into Civil Service of the Empire come from Earth, or from the close-in planets of Proxima and Alpha Centaurus. They go out unmarried, and they stay that way, or marry women native to the planets where they are sent.

But Joanna Magnusson was one of the rare Earth women who had come out with her husband, twenty years ago. There are two kinds of Earthwomen like that. They make their quarterings a little bit of home, or a little bit of hell. Joanna had made their house look like a transported corner of Earth.

I never knew quite what to think of the Magnusson household. It seemed to me almost madness to live under a red sun, yet come inside to yellow light, to live on a world with the wild beauty of Wolf and yet live as they might have lived on their home planet. Or maybe I was the one who was out of step. I had done the reprehensible thing they called "going native." Possibly I had done just that, and in absorbing myself into the new world, had lost the ability to fit into the old.

Joanna, a chubby comfortable woman in her forties, opened the door and gave me her hand. "Come in, Race. Juli's expecting you."

"It's good of you." I broke off, unable to express my gratitude. Juli and I had come from Earth—our father had been an officer on the old starship Landfall when Juli was only a child. He had died in a wreck off Procyon, and Mack Magnusson had found me a place in Intelligence because I spoke four of the Wolf languages and haunted the Kharsa with Rakhal whenever I could get away.

They had also taken Juli into their own home, like a younger sister. They hadn't said much—because they had liked Rakhal—when the breakup came. But that terrible night when Rakhal and I nearly killed each other, and Rakhal came with his face bleeding and took Juli away with him, had hurt them hard. Yet it had made them all the kinder to me.

Joanna said forthrightly, "Nonsense, Race! What else could we do?" She drew me along the hall. "You can talk in here."

I delayed a minute before going through the door she indicated. "How is Juli?"

"Better, I think. I put her to bed in Meta's room, and she slept most of the day. She'll be all right. I'll leave you to talk." Joanna opened the door, and went away.

Juli was awake and dressed, and already some of the terrible frozen horror was gone from her face. She was still tense and devil-ridden, but not hysterical now.

The room, one of the children's bedrooms, wasn't a big one. Even at the top of the Secret Service, a cop doesn't live too well. Not on Terra's Civil Service pay scale. Not, with five youngsters. It looked as if all five of the kids had taken it to pieces, one at a time.

I sat down on a too-low chair and said, "Juli, we haven't much time, I've got to be out of the city before dark. I want to know about Rakhal, what he does, what he's like now. Remember, I haven't seen him for years. Tell me everything—his friends, his amusements, everything you know."

"I always thought you knew him better than I did." Juli had a fidgety little way of coiling the links of the chain around her wrists and it made me nervous.

"It's routine, Juli. Police work. Mostly I play by ear, but I try to start out by being methodical."

She answered everything I asked her, but the sum total wasn't much and it wouldn't help much. As I said, it's easy to disappear on Wolf. Juli knew he had been friendly with the new holders of the Great House on Shainsa, but she didn't even know their name.

I heard one of the Magnusson children fly to the street door and return, shouting for her mother. Joanna knocked at the door of the room and came in.

"There's a chak outside who wants to see you, Race."

I nodded. "Probably my fancy dress. Can I change in the back room, Joanna? Will you keep my clothes here till I get back?"

I went to the door and spoke to the furred nonhuman in the sibilant jargon of the Kharsa and he handed me what looked like a bundle of rags. There were hard lumps inside. The chak said softly, "I hear a rumor in the Kharsa, Raiss. Perhaps it will help you. Three men from Shainsa are in the city. They came here to seek a woman who has vanished, and a toymaker. They are returning at sunrise. Perhaps you can arrange to travel in their caravan."

I thanked him and carried the bundle inside. In the empty back room I stripped to the skin and unrolled the bundle. There was a pair of baggy striped breeches, a worn and shabby shirtcloak with capacious pockets, a looped belt with half the gilt rubbed away and the base metal showing through, and a scuffed pair of ankle-boots tied with frayed thongs of different colors. There was a little cluster of amulets and seals. I chose two or three of the commonest kind, and strung them around my neck.

One of the lumps in the bundle was a small jar, holding nothing but the ordinary spices sold in the market, with which the average Dry-towner flavors food. I rubbed some of the powder on my body, put a pinch in the pocket of my shirtcloak, and chewed a few of the buds, wrinkling my nose at the long-unfamiliar pungency.

The second lump was a skean, and unlike the worn and shabby garments, this was brand-new and sharp and bright, and its edge held a razor glint. I tucked it into the clasp of my shirtcloak, a reassuring weight. It was the only weapon I could dare to carry.

The last of the solid objects in the bundle was a flat wooden case, about nine by ten inches. I slid it open. It was divided carefully into sections cushioned with sponge-absorbent plastic, and in them lay tiny slips of glass, on Wolf as precious as jewels. They were lenses—camera lenses, microscope lenses, even eyeglass lenses. Packed close, there were nearly a hundred of them nested by the shock-absorbent stuff.

They were my excuse for travel to Shainsa. Over and above the necessities of trade, a few items of Terran manufacture—vacuum tubes, transistors, lenses for cameras and binoculars, liquors and finely forged small tools—are literally worth their weight in platinum.

Even in cities where Terrans have never gone, these things bring exorbitant prices, and trading in them is a Dry-town privilege. Rakhal had been a trader, so Juli told me, in fine wire and surgical instruments. Wolf is not a mechanized planet, and has never developed any indigenous industrial system; the psychology of the nonhuman seldom runs to technological advances.

I went down the hallway again to the room where Juli was waiting. Catching a glimpse in a full-length mirror, I was startled. All traces of the Terran civil servant, clumsy and uncomfortable in his ill-fitting clothes, had dropped away. A Dry-towner, rangy and scarred, looked out at me, and it seemed that the expression on his face was one of amazement.

Joanna whirled as I came into the room and visibly paled before, recovering her self-control, she gave a nervous little giggle. "Goodness, Race, I didn't know you!"

Juli whispered, "Yes, I—I remember you better like that. You're—you look so much like—"

The door flew open and Mickey Magnusson scampered into the room, a chubby little boy browned by a Terra-type sunlamp and glowing with health. In his hand he held some sparkling thing that gave off tiny flashes and glints of color.

I gave the kid a grin before I realized that I was disguised anyhow and probably a hideous sight. The little boy backed off, but Joanna put her plump hand on his shoulder, murmuring soothing things.

Mickey toddled toward Juli, holding up the shining thing in his hands as if to display something very precious and beloved. Juli bent and held out her arms, then her face contracted and she snatched at the plaything.

"Mickey, what's that?"

He thrust it protectively behind his back. "Mine!"

"Mickey, don't be naughty," Joanna chided.

"Please let me see," Juli coaxed, and he brought it out, slowly, still suspicious. It was an angled prism of crystal, star-shaped, set in a frame which could get the star spinning like a solidopic. But it displayed a new and comical face every time it was turned.

Mickey turned it round and round, charmed at being the center of attention. There seemed to be dozens of faces, shifting with each spin of the prism, human and nonhuman, all dim and slightly distorted. My own face, Juli's, Joanna's came out of the crystal surface, not a reflection but a caricature.

A choked sound from Juli made me turn in dismay. She had let herself drop to the floor and was sitting there, white as death, supporting herself with her two hands.

"Race! Find out where he got that—that thing!"

I bent and shook her. "What's the matter with you?" I demanded. She had lapsed into the dazed, sleepwalking horror of this morning. She whispered, "It's not a toy. Rindy had one. Joanna, where did he get it?" She pointed at the shining thing with an expression of horror which would have been laughable had it been less real, less filled with terror.

Joanna cocked her head to one side and wrinkled her forehead, reflectively. "Why, I don't know, now you come to ask me. I thought maybe one of the chaks had given it to Mickey. Bought it in the bazaar, maybe. He loves it. Do get up off the floor, Juli!"

Juli scrambled to her feet. She said, "Rindy had one. It—it terrified me. She would sit and look at it by the hour, and—I told you about it, Race. I threw it out once, and she woke up and screamed. She shrieked for hours and hours and she ran out in the dark and dug for it in the trash pile, where I'd buried it. She went out in the dark, broke all her fingernails, but she dug it out again." She checked herself, staring at Joanna, her eyes wide in appeal.

"Well, dear," said Joanna with mild, rebuking kindness, "you needn't be so upset. I don't think Mickey's so attached to it as all that, and anyhow I'm not going to throw it away." She patted Juli reassuringly on the shoulder, then gave Mickey a little shove toward the door and turned to follow him. "You'll want to talk alone before Race leaves. Good luck, wherever you're going, Race." She held out her hand forthrightly.

"And don't worry about Juli," she added in an undertone. "We'll take good care of her."

When I came back to Juli she was standing by the window, looking through the oddly filtered glass that dimmed the red sun to orange. "Joanna thinks I'm crazy, Race."

"She thinks you're upset."

"Rindy's an odd child, a real Dry-towner. But it's not my imagination, Race, it's not. There's something—" Suddenly she sobbed aloud again.

"Homesick, Juli?"

"I was, a little, the first years. But I was happy, believe me." She turned her face to me, shining with tears. "You've got to believe I never regretted it for a minute."

"I'm glad," I said dully. That made it just fine.

"Only that toy—"

"Who knows? It might be a clue to something." The toy had reminded me of something, too, and I tried to remember what it was. I'd seen nonhuman toys in the Kharsa, even bought them for Mack's kids. When a single man is invited frequently to a home with five youngsters, it's about the only way he can repay that hospitality, by bringing the children odd trifles and knicknacks. But I had never seen anything quite like this one, until—

—Until yesterday. The toy-seller they had hunted out of the Kharsa, the one who had fled into the shrine of Nebran and vanished. He had had half a dozen of those prism-and-star sparklers.

I tried to call up a mental picture of the little toy-seller. I didn't have much luck. I'd seen him only in that one swift glance from beneath his hood. "Juli, have you ever seen a little man, like a chak only smaller, twisted, hunchbacked? He sells toys—"

She looked blank. "I don't think so, although there are dwarf chaks in the Polar Cities. But I'm sure I've never seen one."

"It was just an idea." But it was something to think about. A toy-seller had vanished. Rakhal, before disappearing, had smashed all Rindy's toys. And the sight of a plaything of cunningly-cut crystal had sent Juli into hysterics.

"I'd better go before it's too dark," I said. I buckled the final clasp of my shirtcloak, fitted my skean another notch into it, and counted the money Mack had advanced me for expenses. "I want to get into the Kharsa and hunt up the caravan to Shainsa."

"You're going there first?"

"Where else?"

Juli turned, leaning one hand against the wall. She looked frail and ill, years older than she was. Suddenly she flung her thin arms around me, and a link of the chain on her fettered hands struck me hard, as she cried out, "Race, Race, he'll kill you! How can I live with that on my conscience too?"

"You can live with a hell of a lot on your conscience." I disengaged her arms firmly from my neck. A link of the chain caught on the clasp of my shirtcloak, and again something snapped inside me. I grasped the chain in my two hands and gave a mighty heave, bracing my foot against the wall. The links snapped asunder. A flying end struck Juli under the eye. I ripped at the seals of the jeweled cuffs, tore them from her arms, find threw the whole assembly into a corner, where it fell with a clash.

"Damn it," I roared, "that's over! You're never going to wear those things again!" Maybe after six years in the Dry-towns, Juli was beginning to guess what those six years behind a desk had meant to me.

"Juli, I'll find your Rindy for you, and I'll bring Rakhal in alive. But don't ask more than that. Just alive. And don't ask me how."

He'd be alive when I got through with him. Sure, he'd be alive.

Just.

Chapter Five

It was getting dark when I slipped through a side gate, shabby and inconspicuous, into the spaceport square. Beyond the yellow lamps, I knew that the old city was beginning to take on life with the falling night. Out of the chinked pebble-houses, men and woman, human and nonhuman, came forth into the moonlit streets.

If anyone noticed me cross the square, which I doubted, they took me for just another Dry-town vagabond, curious about the world of the strangers from beyond the stars, and who, curiosity satisfied, was drifting back where he belonged. I turned down one of the dark alleys that led away, and soon was walking in the dark.

The Kharsa was not unfamiliar to me as a Terran, but for the last six years I had seen only its daytime face. I doubted if there were a dozen Earthmen in the Old Town tonight, though I saw one in the bazaar, dirty and lurching drunk; one of those who run renegade and homeless between worlds, belonging to neither. This was what I had nearly become.

I went further up the hill with the rising streets. Once I turned, and saw below me the bright-lighted spaceport, the black many-windowed loom of the skyscraper like a patch of alien shadow in the red-violet moonlight. I turned my back on them and walked on.

At the fringe of the thieves market I paused outside a wineshop where Dry-towners were made welcome. A golden nonhuman child murmured something as she pattered by me in the street, and I stopped, gripped by a spasm of stagefright. Had the dialect of Shainsa grown rusty on my tongue? Spies were given short shrift on Wolf, and a mile from the spaceport, I might as well have been on one of those moons. There were no spaceport shockers at my back now. And someone might remember the tale of an Earthman with a scarred face who had gone to Shainsa in disguise....

I shrugged the shirtcloak around my shoulders, pushed the door and went in. I had remembered that Rakhal was waiting for me. Not beyond this door, but at the end of the trail, behind some other door, somewhere. And we have a byword in Shainsa: A trail without beginning has no end.

Right there I stopped thinking about Juli, Rindy, the Terran Empire, or what Rakhal, who knew too many of Terra's secrets, might do if he had turned renegade. My fingers went up and stroked, musingly, the ridge of scar tissue along my mouth. At that moment I was thinking only of Rakhal, of an unsettled blood-feud, and of my revenge.

Red lamps were burning inside the wineshop, where men reclined on frowsy couches. I stumbled over one of them, found an empty place and let myself sink down on it, arranging myself automatically in the sprawl of Dry-towners indoors. In public they stood, rigid and formal, even to eat and drink. Among themselves, anything less than a loose-limbed sprawl betrayed insulting watchfulness; only a man who fears secret murder keeps himself on guard.

A girl with a tangled rope of hair down her back came toward me. Her hands were unchained, meaning she was a woman of the lowest class, not worth safeguarding. Her fur smock was shabby and matted with filth. I sent her for wine. When it came it was surprisingly good, the sweet and treacherous wine of Ardcarran. I sipped it slowly, looking round.

If a caravan for Shainsa were leaving tomorrow, it would be known here. A word dropped that I was returning there would bring me, by ironbound custom, an invitation to travel in their company.

When I sent the woman for wine a second time, a man on a nearby couch got up, and walked over to me.

He was tall even for a Dry-towner, and there was something vaguely familiar about him. He was no riffraff of the Kharsa, either, for his shirtcloak was of rich silk interwoven with metallic threads, and crusted with heavy embroideries. The hilt of his skean was carved from a single green gem. He stood looking down at me for some time before he spoke.

"I never forget a voice, although I cannot bring your face to mind. Have I a duty toward you?"

I had spoken a jargon to the girl, but he addressed me in the lilting, sing-song speech of Shainsa. I made no answer, gesturing him to be seated. On Wolf, formal courtesy requires a series of polite non sequiturs, and while a direct question merely borders on rudeness, a direct answer is the mark of a simpleton.

"A drink?"

"I joined you unasked," he retorted, and summoned the tangle-headed girl. "Bring us better wine than this swill!"

With that word and gesture I recognized him and my teeth clamped hard on my lip. This was the loudmouth who had shown fight in the spaceport cafe, and run away before the dark girl with the sign of Nebran sprawled on her breast.

But in this poor light he had not recognized me. I moved deliberately into the full red glow. If he did not know me for the Terran he had challenged last night in the spaceport cafe, it was unlikely that anyone else would. He stared at me for some minutes, but in the end he only shrugged and poured wine from the bottle he had ordered.

Three drinks later I knew that his name was Kyral and that he was a trader in wire and fine steel tools through the nonhuman towns. And I had given him the name I had chosen, Rascar.

He asked, "Are you thinking of returning to Shainsa?"

Wary of a trap, I hesitated, but the question seemed harmless, so I only countered, "Have you been long in the Kharsa?"

"Several weeks."

"Trading?"

"No." He applied himself to the wine again. "I was searching for a member of my family."

"Did you find him?"

"Her," said Kyral, and ceremoniously spat. "No, I didn't find her. What is your business in Shainsa?"

I chuckled briefly. "As a matter of fact, I am searching for a member of my family."

He narrowed his eyelids as if he suspected me of mocking him, but personal privacy is the most rigid convention of the Dry-towns and such mockery showed a sensible disregard for prying questions if I did not choose to answer them. He questioned no further.

"I can use an extra man to handle the loads. Are you good with pack animals? If so, you are welcome to travel under the protection of my caravan."

I agreed. Then, reflecting that Juli and Rakhal must, after all, be known in Shainsa, I asked, "Do you know a trader who calls himself Sensar?"

He started slightly; I saw his eyes move along my scars. Then reserve, like a lowered curtain, shut itself over his face, concealing a brief satisfied glimmer. "No," he lied, and stood up.

"We leave at first daylight. Have your gear ready." He flipped something at me, and I caught it in midair. It was a stone incised with Kyral's name in the ideographs of Shainsa. "You can sleep with the caravan if you care to. Show that token to Cuinn."

Kyral's caravan was encamped in a barred field past the furthest gates of the Kharsa. About a dozen men were busy loading the pack animals—horses shipped in from Darkover, mostly. I asked the first man I met for Cuinn. He pointed out a burly fellow in a shiny red shirtcloak, who was busy at chewing out one of the young men for the way he'd put a packsaddle on his beast.

Shainsa is a good language for cursing, but Cuinn had a special talent at it. I blinked in admiration while I waited for him to get his breath so I could hand him Kyral's token.

In the light of the fire I saw what I'd half expected: he was the second of the Dry-towners who'd tried to rough me up in the spaceport cafe. Cuinn barely glanced at the cut stone and tossed it back, pointing out one of the packhorses. "Load your personal gear on that one, then get busy and show this mush-headed wearer of sandals"—an insult carrying particularly filthy implications in Shainsa—"how to fasten a packstrap."

He drew breath and began to swear at the luckless youngster again, and I relaxed. He evidently hadn't recognized me, either. I took the strap in my hand, guiding it through the saddle loop. "Like that," I told the kid, and Cuinn stopped swearing long enough to give me a curt nod of acknowledgment and point out a heap of boxed and crated objects.

"Help him load up. We want to get clear of the city by daybreak," he ordered, and went off to swear at someone else.

Kyral turned up at dawn, and a few minutes later the camp had vanished into a small scattering of litter and we were on our way.

Kyral's caravan, in spite of Cuinn's cursing, was well-managed and well-handled. The men were Dry-towners, eleven of them, silent and capable and most of them very young. They were cheerful on the trail, handled the pack animals competently, during the day, and spent most of the nights grouped around the fire, gambling silently on the fall of the cut-crystal prisms they used for dice.

Three days out of the Kharsa I began to worry about Cuinn.

It was of course a spectacular piece of bad luck to find all three of the men from the spaceport cafe in Kyral's caravan. Kyral had obviously not known me, and even by daylight he paid no attention to me except to give an occasional order. The second of the three was a gangling kid who probably never gave me a second look, let alone a third.

But Cuinn was another matter. He was a man my own age, and his fierce eyes had a shrewdness in them that I did not trust. More than once I caught him watching me, and on the two or three occasions when he drew me into conversation, I found his questions more direct than Dry-town good manners allowed. I weighed the possibility that I might have to kill him before we reached Shainsa.

We crossed the foothills and began to climb upward toward the mountains. The first few days I found myself short of breath as we worked upward into thinner air, then my acclimatization returned and I began to fall into the pattern of the days and nights on the trail. The Trade City was still a beacon in the night, but its glow on the horizon grew dimmer with each day's march.

Higher we climbed, along dangerous trails where men had to dismount and let the pack animals pick their way, foot by foot. Here in these altitudes the sun at noonday blazed redder and brighter, and the Dry-towners, who come from the parched lands in the sea-bottoms, were burned and blistered by the fierce light. I had grown up under the blazing sun of Terra, and a red sun like Wolf, even at its hottest, caused me no discomfort. This alone would have made me suspect. Once again I found Cuinn's fierce eyes watching me.

As we crossed the passes and began to descend the long trail through the thick forests, we got into nonhuman country. Racing against the Ghost Wind, we skirted the country around Charin, and the woods inhabited by the terrible Ya-men, birdlike creatures who turn cannibal when the Ghost Wind blows.

Later the trail wound through thicker forests of indigo trees and grayish-purple brushwood, and at night we heard the howls of the catmen of these latitudes. At night we set guards about the caravan, and the dark spaces and shadows were filled with noises and queer smells and rustlings.

Nevertheless, the day's marches and the night watches passed without event until the night I shared guard with Cuinn. I had posted myself at the edge of the camp, the fire behind me. The men were sleeping rolls of snores, huddled close around the fire. The animals, hobbled with double ropes, front feet to hind feet, shifted uneasily and let out long uncanny whines.

I heard Cuinn pacing behind me. I heard a rustle at the edge of the forest, a stir and whisper beyond the trees, and turned to speak to him, then saw him slipping away toward the outskirts of the clearing.

For a moment I thought nothing of it, thinking that he was taking a few steps toward the gap in the trees where he had disappeared. I suppose I had the idea that he had slipped away to investigate some noise or shadow, and that I should be at hand.

Then I saw the flicker of lights beyond the trees—light from the lantern Cuinn had been carrying in his hand! He was signaling!

I slipped the safety clasp from the hilt of my skean and went after him. In the dimming glow of the fire I fancied I saw luminous eyes watching me, and the skin on my back crawled. I crept up behind him and leaped. We went down in a tangle of flailing legs and arms, and in less than a second he had his skean out and I was gripping his wrist, trying desperately to force the blade away from my throat.

I gasped, "Don't be a fool! One yell and the whole camp will be awake! Who were you signaling?"

In the light of the fallen lantern, lips drawn back in a snarl, he looked almost inhuman. He strained at the knife for a moment, then dropped it. "Let me up," he said.

I got up and kicked the fallen skean toward him. "Put that away. What in hell were you doing, trying to bring the catmen down on us?"

For a moment he looked taken aback, then his fierce face closed down again and he said wrathfully, "Can't a man walk away from the camp without being half strangled?"

I glared at him, but realized I really had nothing to go by. He might have been answering a call of nature, and the movement of the lantern accidental. And if someone had jumped me from behind, I might have pulled a knife on him myself. So I only said, "Don't do it again. We're all too jumpy."

There were no other incidents that night, or the next. The night after, while I lay huddled in my shirtcloak and blanket by the fire, I saw Cuinn slip out of his bedroll and steal away. A moment later there was a gleam in the darkness, but before I could summon the resolve to get up and face it out with him, he returned, looked cautiously at the snoring men, and crawled back into his blankets.

While we were unpacking at the next camp, Kyral halted beside me. "Heard anything queer lately? I've got the notion we're being trailed. We'll be out of these forests tomorrow, and after that it's clear road all the way to Shainsa. If anything's going to happen, it will happen tonight."

I debated speaking to him about Cuinn's signals. No, I had my own business waiting for me in Shainsa. Why mix myself up in some other, private intrigue?

He said, "I'm putting you and Cuinn on watch again. The old men doze off, and the young fellows get to daydreaming or fooling around. That's all right most of the time, but I want someone who'll keep his eyes open tonight. Did you ever know Cuinn before this?"

"Never set eyes on him."

"Funny, I had the notion—" He shrugged, turned away, then stopped.

"Don't think twice about rousing the camp if there's any disturbance. Better a false alarm than an ambush that catches us all in our blankets. If it came to a fight, we might be in a bad way. We all carry skeans, but I don't think there's a shocker in the whole camp, let alone a gun. You don't have one by any chance?"

After the men had turned in, Cuinn patrolling the camp, halted a minute beside me and cocked his head toward the rustling forest.

"What's going on in there?"

"Who knows? Catmen on the prowl, probably, thinking the horses would make a good meal, or maybe that we would."

"Think it will come to a fight?"

"I wouldn't know."

He surveyed me for a moment without speaking. "And if it did?"

"We'd fight." Then I sucked in my breath, for Cuinn had spoken Terran Standard, and I, without thinking had answered in the same language. He grinned, showing white teeth filed to a point.

"I thought so!"

I seized his shoulder and demanded roughly, "And what are you going to do about it?"

"That depends on you," he answered, "and what you want in Shainsa. Tell me the truth. What were you doing in the Terran Zone?" He gave me no chance to answer. "You know who Kyral is, don't you?"

"A trader," I said, "who pays my wages and minds his own affairs." I moved backward, hand on my skean, braced for a sudden rush. He made no aggressive motion, however.

"Kyral told me you'd been asking questions about Rakhal Sensar," he said. "Clever. Now I, for one, could have told you he'd never set eyes on Rakhal. I—"

He broke off, hearing a noise in the forest, a long eerie howl. I muttered, "If you've brought them down on us—"

He shook his head urgently. "I had to take that chance, to get word to the others. It won't work. Where's the girl?"

I hardly heard him. I was hearing twigs snap, and silent sneaking feet. I turned for a yell that would rouse the camp and Cuinn grabbed me hard, saying insistently, "Quick! Where's the girl! Go back and tell her it won't work! If Kyral suspected—"

He never finished the sentence. Just behind us came another of the long eerie howls. I knocked Cuinn away, and suddenly the night was filled with crouching forms that came down on us like a whirlwind.

I shouted madly as the camp came alive with men struggling out of blankets, fighting for life itself. I ran hard, still shouting, for the enclosure where we had tied the horses. A catman, slim and black-furred, was crouched and cutting the hobble-strings of the nearest animal. I hurled myself on him. He exploded, clawing, raking my shoulder with talons that ripped the rough cloth like paper. I whipped out my skean and slashed upward. The talons contracted in my shoulder and I gasped with pain. Then the thing howled and fell away, clawing at the air. It twitched and lay still.

Four shots in rapid succession cracked in the clearing. Kyral to the contrary, someone must have had a pistol. I heard one of the cat-things wail, a hoarse dying rattle. Something dark clawed my arm and I slashed with the knife, going down as another set of talons fastened in my back, rolling and clutching.

I managed to get the thing's forelimbs wedged under my elbow, my knee in its spine. I heaved, bent it backward, backward till it screamed, a high wail.

Then I felt the spine snap and the dead thing mewled once, just air escaping from collapsing lungs, and slid limp from my thigh. Erect it had not been over four feet tall and in the light of the dying fire it might have been a dead lynx.

"Rascar...." I heard a gasp, a groan. I whirled and saw Kyral go down, struggling, drowning in half a dozen or more of the fierce half-humans. I leaped at the smother of bodies, ripped one away with a stranglehold, slashed at its throat.

They were easy to kill.

I heard a high, urgent scream in their mewing tongue. Then the furred black things seemed to melt into the forest as silently as they had come. Kyral, dazed, his forehead running blood, his arm slashed to the bone, was sitting on the ground, still stunned.

Somebody had to take charge. I bellowed, "Lights! Get lights. They won't come back if we have enough light, they can only see well in the dark."

Someone stirred the fire. It blazed up as they piled on dead branches, and I roughly commanded one of the kids to fill every lantern he could find, and get them burning. Four of the dead things were lying in the clearing. The youngster I'd helped loading horses, the first day, gazed down at one of the catmen, half-disemboweled by somebody's skean, and suddenly bolted for the bushes, where I heard him retching.

I set the others with stronger stomachs to dragging the bodies away from the clearing, and went back to see how badly Kyral was hurt. He had the rip in his arm and his face was covered with blood from a shallow scalp wound, but he insisted on getting up to inspect the hurts of the others.

There was no one without a claw-wound in leg or back or shoulder, but none were serious, and we were all feeling fairly cheerful when someone demanded, "Where's Cuinn?"

He didn't seem to be anywhere. Kyral, staggering slightly, insisted on searching, but I felt we wouldn't find him. "He probably went off with his friends," I snorted, and told about the signaling. Kyral looked grave.

"You should have told me," he began, but shouts from the far end of the clearing sent us racing there. We nearly stumbled over a single, solitary, motionless form, outstretched and lifeless, blind eyes staring upward at the moons.

It was Cuinn. And his throat had been torn completely out.

Chapter Six

Once we were free of the forest, the road to the Dry-towns lay straight before us, with no hidden dangers. Some of us limped for a day or two, or favored an arm or leg clawed by the catmen, but I knew that what Kyral said was true; it was a lucky caravan which had to fight off only one attack.

Cuinn haunted me. A night or two of turning over his cryptic words in my mind had convinced me that whoever, or whatever he'd been signaling, it wasn't the catmen. And his urgent question "Where's the girl?" swam endlessly in my brain, making no more sense than when I had first heard it. Who had he mistaken me for? What did he think I was mixed up in? And who, above all, were the "others" who had to be signaled, at the risk of an attack by catmen which had meant his own death?

With Cuinn dead, and Kyral thinking I'd saved his life, a large part of the responsibility for the caravan now fell on me. And strangely I enjoyed it, making the most of this interval when I was separated from the thought of blood-feud or revenge, the need of spying or the threat of exposure. During those days and nights on the trail I grew back slowly into the Dry-towner I once had been. I knew I would be sorry when the walls of Shainsa rose on the horizon, bringing me back inescapably to my own quest.

We swung wide, leaving the straight trail to Shainsa, and Kyral announced his intention of stopping for half a day at Canarsa, one of the walled nonhuman cities which lay well off the traveled road. To my inadvertent show of surprise, he returned that he had trading connections there.

"We all need a day's rest, and the Silent Ones will buy from me, though they have few dealings with men. Look here, I owe you something. You have lenses? You can get a better price in Canarsa than you'd get in Ardcarran or Shainsa. Come along with me, and I'll vouch for you."

Kyral had been most friendly since the night I had dug him out from under the catmen, and I knew no way to refuse without exposing myself for the sham trader I was. But I was deathly apprehensive. Even with Rakhal I had never entered any of the nonhuman towns.

On Wolf, human and nonhuman have lived side by side for centuries. And the human is not always the superior being. I might pass, among the Dry-towners and the relatively stupid humanoid chaks, for another Dry-towner. But Rakhal had cautioned me I could not pass among nonhumans for native Wolfan, and warned me against trying.

Nevertheless, I accompanied Kyral, carrying the box which had cost about a week's pay in the Terran Zone and was worth a small fortune in the Dry-towns.

Canarsa seemed, inside the gates, like any other town. The houses were round, beehive fashion, and the streets totally empty. Just inside the gates a hooded figure greeted us, and gestured us by signs to follow him. He was covered from head to foot with some coarse and shiny fiber woven into stuff that looked like sacking.

But under the thick hooding was horror. It slithered and it had nothing like a recognizable human shape or walk, and I felt the primeval ape in me cowering and gibbering in a corner of my brain. Kyral muttered, close to my ear, "No outsider is ever allowed to look on the Silent Ones in their real form. I think they're deaf and dumb, but be damn careful."

"You bet," I whispered, and was glad the streets were empty. I walked along, trying not to look at the gliding motion of that shrouded thing up ahead.

The trading was done in an open hut of reeds which looked as if it had been built in a hurry, and was not square, round, hexagonal or any other recognizable geometrical shape. It formed a pattern of its own, presumably, but my human eyes couldn't see it. Kyral said in a breath of a whisper, "They'll tear it down and burn it after we leave. We're supposed to have contaminated it too greatly for any of the Silent Ones ever to enter again. My family has traded with them for centuries, and we're almost the only ones who have ever entered the city."

Then two of the Silent Ones of Canarsa, also covered with that coarse shiny stuff, slithered into the hut, and Kyral choked off his words as if he had swallowed them.

It was the strangest trading I had ever done. Kyral laid out the small forged-steel tools and the coils of thin fine wire, and I unpacked my lenses and laid them out in neat rows. The Silent Ones neither spoke nor moved, but through a thin place in the gray veiling I saw a speck which might have been a phosphorescent eye, moving back and forth as if scanning the things laid out for their inspection.

Then I smothered a gasp, for suddenly blank spaces appeared in the rows of merchandise. Certain small tools—wirecutters, calipers, surgical scissors—had vanished, and all the coils of wire had disappeared. Blanks equally had appeared in the rows of lenses; all of my tiny, powerful microscope lenses had vanished. I cast a quick glance at Kyral, but he seemed unsurprised. I recalled vague rumors of the Silent Ones, and concluded that, eerie though it seemed, this was merely their way of doing business.

Kyral pointed at one of the tools, at an exceptionally fine pair of binocular lenses, at the last of the coils of wire. The shrouded ones did not move, but the lenses and the wire vanished. The small tool remained, and after a moment Kyral dropped his hand.

I took my cue from Kyral and remained motionless, awaiting whatever surprise was coming. I had halfway expected what happened next. In the blank spaces, little points of light began to glimmer, and after a moment, blue and red and green gem-stones appeared there. To me the substitution appeared roughly equitable and fair, though I am no judge of the fine points of gems.

Kyral scowled slightly and pointed to one of the green gems, and after a moment it whisked away and a blue one took its place. In another spot where a fine set of surgical instruments had lain, Kyral pointed at the blue gem which now lay there, shook his head and held out three fingers. After a moment, a second blue stone lay winking beside the first.

Kyral did not move, but inexorably held out the three fingers. There was a little swirling in the air, and then both gems vanished, and the case of surgical instruments lay in their place.

Still Kyral did not move, but held the three fingers out for a full minute. Finally he dropped them and bent to pick up the case instruments. Again the little swirl in the air, and the instruments vanished. In their place lay three of the blue gems. My mouth twitched in the first amusement I had felt since we entered this uncanny place. Evidently bargaining with the Silent Ones was not a great deal different than bargaining with anyone anywhere. Nevertheless, under the eyes of those shrouded but horrible forms—if they had eyes, which I doubted—I had no impulse to protest their offered prices.

I gathered up the rejected lenses, repacked them neatly, and helped Kyral recrate the tools and instruments the Silent Ones had not wanted. I noticed that in addition to the microscope lenses and surgical instruments, they had taken all the fine wire. I couldn't imagine, and didn't particularly want to imagine, what they intended to do with it.

On our way back through the streets, unshepherded this time, Kyral's tongue was loosened as if with a great release from tension. "They're psychokinetics," he told me. "Quite a few of the nonhuman races are. I guess they have to be, having no eyes and no hands. But sometimes I wonder if we of the Dry-towns ought to deal with them at all."

"What do you mean?" I asked, not really listening. I was thinking mostly about the way the small objects had melted away and reappeared. The sight had stirred some uncomfortable memory, a vague sense of danger. It was not tangible enough for me to know why I feared it, but just a subliminal uneasiness that kept prodding at me, like a tooth that isn't quite aching yet.

Kyral said, "We of Shainsa live between fire and flood. Terra on the one hand, and on the other maybe something worse, who knows? We know so little about the Silent Ones, and those like them. Who knows, maybe we're giving them the weapons to destroy us—" He broke off, with a gasp, and stood staring down one of the streets.

It lay open and bare between two rows of round houses, and Kyral was staring fixedly at a doorway which had opened there. I followed his paralyzed gaze, and saw the girl.

Hair like spun black glass fell in hard waves around her shoulders, and the red eyes smiled with alien malice, alien mischief, beneath the dark crown of little stars. And the Toad God sprawled in hideous embroideries across the white folds of her breast.

Kyral gulped hoarsely. His hand flew up as he clutched the charms strung about his neck. I imitated the gesture mechanically, watching Kyral, wondering if he would turn and run again. But he stood frozen for a minute. Then the spell broke and he took one step toward the girl, arms outstretched.

"Miellyn!" he cried, and there was heartbreak in his voice. And again, the cry making ringing echoes in the strange street:

"Miellyn! Miellyn!"

This time it was the girl who whirled and fled. Her white robes fluttered and I saw the twinkle of her flying feet as she vanished into a space between the houses and was gone.

Kyral took one blind step down the street, then another. But before he could burst into a run I had him by the arm, dragging him back to sanity.

"Man, you've gone mad! Chase, in a nonhuman town?"

He struggled for a minute, then, with a harsh sigh, he said, "It's all right, I won't—" and shook loose from my arm.

He did not speak again until we reached the gates of Canarsa and they closed, silently and untouched, behind us. I had forgotten the place already.

I had space only to think of the girl, whose face I had not forgotten since the moment when she saved me and disappeared. Now she had appeared again to Kyral. What did it all mean?

I asked, as we walked toward the camp, "Do you know that girl?" But I knew the question was futile. Kyral's face was closed, conceding nothing, and his friendliness had vanished completely.

He said, "Now I know you. You saved me from the catmen, and again in Canarsa, so my hands are bound from harming you. But it is evil to have dealings with those who have been touched by the Toad God." He spat noisily on the ground, looked at me with loathing, and said, "We will reach Shainsa in three days. Stay away from me."

Chapter Seven

Shainsa, first in the chain of Dry-towns that lie in the bed of a long-dried ocean, is set at the center of a great alkali plain; a dusty, parched city bleached by a million years of sun. The houses are high, spreading buildings with many rooms and wide windows. The poorer sort were made of sun-dried brick, the more imposing being cut from the bleached salt stone of the cliffs that rise behind the city.

News travels fast in the Dry-towns. If Rakhal were in the city, he'd soon know that I was here, and guess who I was or why I'd come. I might disguise myself so that my own sister, or the mother who bore me, would not know me. But I had no illusions about my ability to disguise myself from Rakhal. He had created the disguise that was me.

When the second sun set, red and burning, behind the salt cliffs, I knew he was not in Shainsa, but I stayed on, waiting for something to happen. At night I slept in a cubbyhole behind a wineshop, paying an inordinate price for that very dubious privilege. And every day in the sleepy silence of the blood-red noon I paced the public square of Shainsa.

This went on for four days. No one took the slightest notice of another nameless man in a shabby shirtcloak, without name or identity or known business. No one appeared to see me except the dusty children, with pale fleecy hair, who played their patient games on the windswept curbing of the square. They surveyed my scarred face with neither curiosity or fear, and it occurred to me that Rindy might be such another as these.

If I had still been thinking like an Earthman, I might have tried to question one of the children, or win their confidence. But I had a deeper game in hand.

On the fifth day I was so much a fixture that my pacing went unnoticed even by the children. On the gray moss of the square, a few dried-looking old men, their faces as faded as their shirtcloaks and bearing the knife scars of a hundred forgotten flights, drowsed on the stone benches. And along the flagged walk at the edge of the square, as suddenly as an autumn storm in the salt flats, a woman came walking.

She was tall, with a proud swinging walk, and a metallic clashing kept rhythm to her swift steps. Her arms were fettered, each wrist bound with a jeweled bracelet and the bracelets linked together by a long, silver-gilt chain passed through a silken loop at her waist. From the loop swung a tiny golden padlock, but in the lock stood an even tinier key, signifying that she was a higher caste than her husband or consort, that her fettering was by choice and not command.

She stopped directly before me and raised her arm in formal greeting like a man. The chain made a tinkling sound in the hushed square as her other hand was pulled up tight against the silken loop at her waist. She stood surveying me for some moments, and finally I raised my head and returned her gaze. I don't know why I had expected her to have hair like spun black glass and eyes that burned with a red reflection of the burning star.

This woman's eyes were darker than the poison-berries of the salt cliffs, and her mouth was a cut berry that looked just as dangerous. She was young, the slimness of her shoulders and the narrow steel-chained wrists told me how very young she was, but her face had seen weather and storms, and her dark eyes had weathered worse psychic storms than that. She did not flinch at the sight of my scars, and met my gaze without dropping her eyes.

"You are a stranger. What is your business in Shainsa?"

I met the direct question with the insolence it demanded, hardly moving my lips. "I have come to buy women for the brothels of Ardcarran. Perhaps when washed you might be suitable. Who could arrange for your sale?"

She took the rebuke impassively, though the bitter crimson of her mouth twitched a little in mischief or rage. But she made no sign. The battle was joined between us, and I knew already that it would be fought to the end.

From somewhere in her draperies, something fell to the ground with a little tinkle. But I knew that trick too and I did not move. Finally she went away without bending to retrieve it and when I looked around I saw that all the fleece-haired children had stolen away, leaving their playthings lying on the curbing. But one or two of the gaffers on the stone benches, who were old enough to show curiosity without losing face, were watching me with impassive eyes.

I could have asked the woman's name then, but I held back, knowing it could only lessen the prestige I had gained from the encounter. I glanced down, without seeming to do so, at the tiny mirror which had fallen from the recesses of the fur robe. Her name might have been inscribed on the reverse.

But I left it lying there to be picked up by the children when they returned, and went back to the wineshop. I had accomplished my first objective; if you can't be inconspicuous, be so damned conspicuous that nobody can miss you. And that in itself is a fair concealment. How many people can accurately describe a street riot?

I was finishing off a bad meal with a stone bottle of worse wine when the chak came in, disregarding the proprietor, and made straight for me. He was furred immaculately white. His velvet muzzle was contracted as if the very smells might soil it, and he kept a dainty paw outstretched to ward off accidental contact with greasy counters or tables or tapestries. His fur was scented, and his throat circled with a collar of embroidered silk. This pampered minion surveyed me with the innocent malice of an uninvolved nonhuman for merely human intrigues.

"You are wanted in the Great House of Shanitha, thcarred man." He spoke the Shainsa dialect with an affected lisp. "Will it pleathe you, come wis' me?"

I came, with no more than polite protest, but was startled. I had not expected the encounter to reach the Great House so soon. Shainsa's Great House had changed hands four times since I had last been in Shainsa. I wasn't overly anxious to appear there.

The white chak, as out of place in the rough Dry-town as a jewel in the streets or a raindrop in the desert, led me along a winding boulevard to an outlying district. He made no attempt to engage me in conversation, and indeed I got the distinct impression that this cockscomb of a nonhuman considered me well beneath his notice. He seemed much more aware of the blowing dust in the street, which ruffled and smudged his carefully combed fur.

The Great House was carved from blocks of rough pink basalt, the entry guarded by two great caryatids enwrapped in chains of carved metal, set somehow into the surface of the basalt. The gilt had long ago worn away from the chains so that it alternately gleamed gold or smudged base metal. The caryatids were patient and blind, their jewel-eyes long vanished under a hotter sun than today's.

The entrance hall was enormous. A Terran starship could have stood upright inside it, was my first impression, but I dismissed that thought quickly; any Terran thought was apt to betray me. But the main hall was built on a scale even more huge, and it was even colder than the legendary hell of the chaks. It was far too big for the people in it.

There was a little solar heater in the ceiling, but it didn't help much. A dim glow came from a metal brazier but that didn't help much either. The chak melted into the shadows, and I went down the steps into the hall by myself, feeling carefully for each step with my feet and trying not to seem to be doing so. My comparative night-blindness is the only significant way in which I really differ from a native Wolfan.

There were three men, two women and a child in the room. They were all Dry-towners and had an obscure family likeness, and they all wore rich garments of fur dyed in many colors. One of the men, old and stooped and withered, was doing something to the brazier. A slim boy of fourteen was sitting cross-legged on a pile of cushions in the corner. There was something wrong with his legs.

A girl of ten in a too-short smock that showed long spider-thin legs above her low leather boots was playing with some sort of shimmery crystals, spilling them out into patterns and scooping them up again from the uneven stones of the floor. One of the women was a fat, creased slattern, whose jewels and dyed furs did not disguise her greasy slovenliness.

Her hands were unchained, and she was biting into a fruit which dripped red juice down the rich blue fur of her robe. The old man gave her a look like murder as I came in, and she straightened slightly but did not discard the fruit. The whole room had a curious look of austere, dignified poverty, to which the fat woman was the only discordant note.

But it was the remaining man and woman who drew my attention, so that I noticed the others only peripherally, in their outermost orbit. One was Kyral, standing at the foot of the dais and glowering at me.

The other was the dark-eyed woman I had rebuked today in the public square.

Kyral said, "So it's you." And his voice held nothing. Not rebuke, not friendliness or a lack of it, not even hatred.

Nothing.

There was only one way to meet it. I faced the girl—she was sitting on a thronelike chair next to the fat woman, and looked like a doe next to a pig—and said boldly, "I assume this summons to mean that you informed your kinsmen of my offer."

She flushed, and that was triumph enough. I held back the triumph, however, wary of overconfidence. The gaffer laughed the high cackle of age, and Kyral broke in with a sharp, angry monosyllable by which I knew that my remark had indeed been repeated, and had lost nothing in the telling. But only the line of his jaw betrayed the anger as he said calmly, "Be quiet, Dallisa. Where did you pick this up?"

I said boldly, "The Great House has changed rulers since last I smelled the salt cliffs. Newcomers do not know my name and theirs is unknown to me."

The old gaffer said thinly to Kyral, "Our name has lost kihar. One daughter is lured away by the Toymaker and another babbles with strangers in the square, and a homeless no-good of the streets does not know our name."

My eyes, growing accustomed to the dark blaze of the brazier, saw that Kyral was biting his lip and scowling. Then he gestured to a table where an array of glassware was set, and at the gesture, the white chak came on noiseless feet and poured wine.

"If you have no blood-feud with my family, will you drink with me?"

"I will," I said, relaxing. Even if he had associated the trader with the scarred Earthman of the spaceport, he seemed to have decided to drop the matter. He seemed startled, but he waited until I had lifted the glass and taken a sip. Then, with a movement like lightning, he leaped from the dais and struck the glass from my lips.

I staggered back, wiping my cut mouth, in a split-second juggling possibilities. The insult was terrible and deadly. I could do nothing now but fight. Men had been murdered in Shainsa for far less. I had come to settle one feud, not involve myself in another, but even while these lightning thoughts flickered in my mind, I had whipped out my skean and I was surprised at the shrillness of my own voice.

"You contrive offense beneath your own roof—"

"Spy and renegade!" Kyral thundered. He did not touch his skean. From the table he caught a long four-thonged whip, making it whistle through the air. The long-legged child scuttled backward. I stepped back one pace, trying to conceal my desperate puzzlement. I could not guess what had prompted Kyral's attack, but whatever it was, I must have made some bad mistake and could count myself lucky to get out of there alive.

Kyral's voice perceptibly trembled with rage. "You dare to come into my own home after I have tracked you to the Kharsa and back, blind fool that I was! But now you shall pay."

The whip sang through the air, hissing past my shoulders. I dodged to one side, retreating step by step as Kyral swung the powerful thongs. It cracked again, and a pain like the burning of red-hot irons seared my upper arm. My skean rattled down from numb fingers.

The whip whacked the floor.

"Pick up your skean," said Kyral. "Pick it up if you dare." He poised the lash again.

The fat woman screamed.

I stood rigid, gauging my chances of disarming him with a sudden leap. Suddenly the girl Dallisa leaped from her seat with a harsh musical chiming of chains.

"Kyral, no! No, Kyral!"

He moved slightly, but did not take his eyes from me. "Get back, Dallisa."

"No! Wait!" She ran to him and caught his whip-arm, dragging it down, and spoke to him hurriedly and urgently. Kyral's face changed as she spoke; he drew a long breath and threw the whip down beside my skean on the floor.

"Answer straight, on your life. What are you doing in Shainsa?"

I could hardly take it in that for the moment I was reprieved from sudden death, from being beaten into bloody death there at Kyral's feet. The girl went back to her thronelike chair. Now I must either tell the truth or a convincing lie, and I was lost in a game where I didn't know the rules. The explanation I thought might get me out alive might be the very one which would bring down instant and painful death. Suddenly, with a poignancy that was almost pain, I wished Rakhal were standing here at my side.

But I had to bluff it out alone.

If they had recognized me for Race Cargill, the Terran spy who had often been in Shainsa, they might release me—it was possible, I supposed, that they were Terran sympathizers. On the other hand, Kyral's shouts of "Spy, renegade!" seemed to suggest the opposite.

I stood trying to ignore the searing pain in my lashed arm, but I knew that blood was running hot down my shoulder. Finally I said, "I came to settle blood-feud."

Kyral's lips thinned in what might have been meant for a smile. "You shall, assuredly. But with whom, remains to be seen."

Knowing I had nothing more to lose, I said, "With a renegade called Rakhal Sensar."

Only the old man echoed my words dully, "Rakhal Sensar?"

I felt heartened, seeing I wasn't dead yet.

"I have sworn to kill him."

Kyral suddenly clapped his hands and shouted to the white chak to clean up the broken glass on the floor. He said huskily, "You are not yourself Rakhal Sensar?"

"I told you he wasn't," said Dallisa, high and hysterically. "I told you he wasn't."

"A scarred man, tall—what was I to think?" Kyral sounded and looked badly shaken. He filled a glass himself and handed it to me, saying hoarsely,

"I did not believe even the renegade Rakhal would break the code so far as to drink with me."

"He would not." I could be positive about this. The codes of Terra had made some superficial impress on Rakhal, but down deep his own world held sway. If these men were at blood-feud with Rakhal and he stood here where I stood, he would have let himself be beaten into bloody rags before tasting their wine.

I took the glass, raised it and drained it. Then, holding it out before me, I said, "Rakhal's life is mine. But I swear by the red star and by the unmoving mountains, by the black snow and by the Ghost Wind, I have no quarrel with any beneath this roof." I cast the glass to the floor, where it shattered on the stones.

Kyral hesitated, but under the blazing eyes of the girl he quickly poured himself a glass of the wine and drank a few sips, then flung down the glass. He stepped forward and laid his hands on my shoulders. I winced as he touched the welt of the lash and could not raise my own arm to complete the ceremonial toast.

Kyral stepped away and shrugged. "Shall I have one of the women see to your hurt?" He looked at Dallisa, but she twisted her mouth. "Do it yourself!"

"It is nothing," I said, not truthfully. "But I demand in requital that since we are bound by spilled blood under your roof, that you give me what news you have of Rakhal, the spy and renegade."

Kyral said fiercely, "If I knew, would I be under my own roof?"

The old gaffer on the dais broke into shrill whining laughter. "You have drunk wi' him, Kyral, now he's bound you not to do him harm! I know the story of Rakhal! He was spy for Terra twelve years. Twelve years, and then he fought and flung their filthy money in their faces and left 'em. But his partner was some Dry-town halfbreed or Terran spy and they fought wi' clawed gloves, and near killed one another except the Terrans, who have no honor, stopped 'em. See the marks of the kifirgh on his face!"

"By Sharra the golden-chained," said Kyral, gazing at me with something like a grin. "You are, if nothing else, a very clever man. What are you, spy, or half-caste of some Ardcarran slut?"

"What I am doesn't matter to you," I said. "You have blood-feud with Rakhal, but mine is older than yours and his life is mine. As you are bound in honor to kill"—the formal phrases came easily now to my tongue; the Earthman had slipped away—"so you are bound in honor to help me kill. If anyone beneath your roof knows anything of Rakhal—"

Kyral's smile bared his teeth.

"Rakhal works against the Son of the Ape," he said, using the insulting Wolf term for the Terrans. "If we help you to kill him, we remove a goad from their flanks. I prefer to let the filthy Terranan spend their strength trying to remove it themselves. Moreover, I believe you are yourself an Earthman.

"You have no right to the courtesy I extend to we, the People of the Sky. Yet you have drunk wine with me and I have no quarrel with you." He raised his hand in dismissal, outfencing me. "Leave my roof in safety and my city with honor."

I could not protest or plead. A man's kihar, his personal dignity, is a precious thing in Shainsa, and he had placed me so I could not compromise mine further in words. Yet I lost kihar equally if I left at his bidding, like an inferior dismissed.

One desperate gamble remained.

"A word," I said, raising my hand, and while he half turned, startled, believing I was indeed about to compromise my dignity by a further plea, I flung it at him:

"I will bet shegri with you."

His iron composure looked shaken. I had delivered a blow to his belief that I was an Earthman, for it is doubtful if there are six Earthmen on Wolf who know about shegri, the dangerous game of the Dry-towns.

It is no ordinary gamble, for what the better stakes is his life, possibly his reason. Rarely indeed will a man beg shegri unless he has nothing further to lose.

It is a cruel, possibly decadent game, which has no parallel anywhere in the known universe.

But I had no choice. I had struck a cold trail in Shainsa. Rakhal might be anywhere on the planet and half of Magnusson's month was already up. Unless I could force Kyral to tell what he knew, I might as well quit.

So I repeated: "I will bet shegri with you."

And Kyral stood unmoving.

For what the shegrin wagers is his courage and endurance in the face of torture and an unknown fate. On his side, the stakes are clearly determined beforehand. But if he loses, his punishment or penalty is at the whim of the one who has accepted him, and he may be put to whatever doom the winner determines.

And this is the contest:

The shegrin permits himself to be tortured from sunrise to sunset. If he endures he wins. It is as simple as that. He can stop the torture at any moment by a word, but to do so is a concession of defeat.

This is not as dangerous as it might, at first, seem. The other party to the bet is bound by the ironclad codes of Wolf to inflict no permanent physical damage (no injury that will not heal with three suncourses). But from sunrise to sunset, any torment or painful ingenuity which the half-human mentality of Wolf can devise must be endured.

The man who can outthink the torture of the moment, the man who can hold in his mind the single thought of his goal—that man can claim the stakes he has set, as well as other concessions made traditional.

The silence grew in the hall. Dallisa had straightened and was watching me intently, her lips parted and the tip of a little red tongue visible between her teeth. The only sound was the tiny crunching as the fat woman nibbled at nuts and cast their shells into the brazier. Even the child on the steps had abandoned her game with the crystal dice, and sat looking up at me with her mouth open. Finally Kyral demanded, "Your stakes?"

"Tell me all you know of Rakhal Sensar and keep silence about me in Shainsa."

"By the red shadow," Kyral burst out, "you have courage, Rascar!"

"Say only yes or no!" I retorted.

Rebuked, he fell silent. Dallisa leaned forward and again, for some unknown reason, I thought of a girl with hair like spun black glass.

Kyral raised his hand. "I say no. I have blood-feud with Rakhal and I will not sell his death to another. Further, I believe you are Terran and I will not deal with you. And finally, you have twice saved my life and I would find small pleasure in torturing you. I say no. Drink again with me and we part without a quarrel."

Beaten, I turned to go.

"Wait," said Dallisa.

She stood up and came down from the dais, slowly this time, walking with dignity to the rhythm of her musically clashing chains. "I have a quarrel with this man."

I started to say that I did not quarrel with women, and stopped myself. The Terran concept of chivalry has no equivalent on Wolf.

She looked at me with her dark poison-berry eyes, icy and level and amused, and said, "I will bet shegri with you, unless you fear me, Rascar."

And I knew suddenly that if I lost, I might better have trusted myself to Kyral and his whip, or to the wild beast-things of the mountains.

Chapter Eight

I slept little that night.

There is a tale told in Daillon of a shegri where the challenger was left in a room alone, where he was blindfolded and told to await the beginning of the torment.

Somewhere in those dark hours of waiting, between the unknown and the unexpected, the hours of telling over to himself the horrors of past shegri, the torture of anticipation alone became the unbearable. A little past noon he collapsed in screams of horror and died raving, unmarred, untouched.

Daybreak came slowly, and with the first streamers of light came Dallisa and the white chak, maliciously uninvolved, sniffing his way through the shabby poverty of the great hall. They took me to a lower dungeon where the slant of the sunlight was less visible. Dallisa said, "The sun has risen."

I said nothing. Any word may be interpreted as a confession of defeat. I resolved to give them no excuse. But my skin crawled and I had that peculiar prickling sensation where the hair on my forearms was bristling erect with tension and fear.

Dallisa said to the chak, "His gear was not searched. See that he has swallowed no anesthetic drugs."

Briefly I gave her credit for thoroughness, even while I wondered in a split second why I had not thought of this. Drugs could blur consciousness, at least, or suspend reality. The white nonhuman sprang forward and pinioned my arms with one strong, spring-steel forearm. With his other hand he forced my jaws open. I felt the furred fingers at the back of my throat, gagged, struggled briefly and doubled up in uncontrollable retching.

Dallisa's poison-berry-eyes regarded me levelly as I struggled upright, fighting off the dizzy sickness of disgust. Something about her impassive face stopped me cold. I had been, momentarily, raging with fury and humiliation. Now I realized that this had been a calculated, careful gesture to make me lose my temper and thus sap my resistance.

If she could set me to fighting, if she could make me spend my strength in rage, my own imagination would fight on her side to make me lose control before the end. Swimming in the glare of her eyes, I realized she had never thought for a moment that I had taken any drug. Acting on Kyral's hint that I was a Terran, she was taking advantage of the well-known Terran revulsion for the nonhuman.

"Blindfold him," Dallisa commanded, then instantly countermanded that: "No, strip him first."

The chak ripped off shirtcloak, shirt, shoes, breeches, and I had my first triumph when the wealed clawmarks on my shoulders—worse, if possible, than those which disfigured my face—were laid bare. The chak screwed up his muzzle in fastidious horror, and Dallisa looked shaken. I could almost read her thoughts:

If he endured this, what hope have I to make him cry mercy?

Briefly I remembered the months I lay feverish and half dead, waiting for the wounds Rakhal had inflicted to heal, those months when I had believed that nothing would ever hurt me again, that I had known the worst of all suffering. But I had been younger then.

Dallisa had picked up two small sharp knives. She weighed them, briefly, gesturing to the chak. Without resisting, I let myself be manhandled backward, spreadeagled against the wall.

Dallisa commanded, "Drive the knives through his palms to the wall!"

My hands twitched convulsively, anticipating the slash of steel, and my throat closed in spasmodic dread. This was breaking the compact, bound as they were not to inflict physical damage. I opened my lips to protest this breaking of the bond of honor and met her dark blazing stare, and suddenly the sweat broke out on my forehead. I had placed myself wholly in their hands, and as Kyral had said, they were in no way bound by honor to respect a pledge to a Terran!

Then, as my hands clenched into fists, I forced myself to relax. This was a bluff, a mental trick to needle me into breaking the pact and pleading for mercy. I set my lips, spread my palms wide against the wall and waited impassively.

She said in her lilting voice, "Take care not to sever the tendons, or his hands would be paralyzed and he may claim we have broken our compact."

The points of the steel, razor-sharp, touched my palms, and I felt blood run down my hand before the pain. With an effort that turned my face white, I did not pull away from the point. The knives drove deeper.

Dallisa gestured to the chak. The knives dropped. Two pinpricks, a quarter of an inch deep, stung in my palm. I had outbluffed her. Had I?

If I had expected her to betray disappointment—and I had—I was disappointed. Abruptly, as if the game had wearied her already, she gestured, and I could not hold back a gasp as my arms were hauled up over my head, twisted violently around one another and trussed with thin cords that bit deep into the flesh. Then the rough upward pull almost jerked my shoulders from their sockets and I heard the giant chak grunt with effort as I was hauled upward until my feet barely, on tiptoe, touched the floor.

"Blindfold him," said Dallisa languidly, "so that he cannot watch the ascent of the sun or its descent or know what is to come."

A dark softness muffled my eyes. After a little I heard her steps retreating. My arms, wrenched overhead and numbed with the bite of the cords, were beginning to hurt badly now. But it wasn't too bad. Surely she did not mean that this should be all....

Sternly I controlled my imagination, taking a tight rein on my thoughts. There was only one way to meet this—hanging blind and racked in space, my toes barely scrabbling at the floor—and that was to take each thing as it came and not look ahead for an instant. First of all I tried to get my feet under me, and discovered that by arching upwards to my fullest height I could bear my weight on tiptoe and ease, a little, the dislocating ache in my armpits by slackening the overhead rope.

But after a little, a cramping pain began to flare through the arches of my feet, and it became impossible to support my weight on tiptoe. I jarred down with violent strain on my wrists and wrenched shoulders again, and for a moment the shooting agony was so intense that I nearly screamed. I thought I heard a soft breath near me.

After a little it subsided to a sharp ache, then to a dull ache, and then to the violent cramping pain again, and once more I struggled to get my toes under me. I realized that by allowing my toes barely to touch the floor they had doubled and tripled the pain by the tantalizing hope of, if not momentary relief, at least the alteration of one pain for another.

I haven't the faintest idea, even now, how long I repeated that agonizing cycle: struggle for a toehold on rough stone, scraping my bare feet raw; arch upward with all my strength to release for a few moments the strain on my wrenched shoulders; the momentary illusion of relief as I found my balance and the pressure lightened on my wrists.

Then the slow creeping, first of an ache, then of a pain, then of a violent agony in the arches of feet and calves. And, delayed to the last endurable moment, that final terrible anguish when the drop of my full weight pulled shoulder and wrist and elbow joints with that bone-shattering jerk.

I started once to estimate how much time had passed, how many hours had crawled by, then checked myself, for that was imminent madness. But once the process had begun my brain would not abandon and I found myself, with compulsive precision, counting off the seconds and the minutes in each cycle: stretch upward, release the pressure on the arms; the beginning of pain in calves and arches and toes; the creeping of pain up ribs and loins and shoulders; the sudden jarring drop on the arms again.

My throat was intolerably dry. Under other circumstances I might have estimated the time by the growth of hunger and thirst, but the rough treatment I had received made this impossible. There were other, unmentionable, humiliating pains.

After a time, to bolster my flagging courage, I found myself thinking of all the ways it might have been worse. I had heard of a shegrin exposed to the bite of poisonous—not fatal, but painfully poisonous—insects, and to the worrying of the small gnawing rodents which can be trained to bite and tear. Or I might have been branded....

I banished the memory with the powerful exorcism; the man in Daillon whose anticipation, alone, of a torture which never came, had broken his mind. There was only one way to conquer this, and that was to act as if the present moment was the only one, and never for a moment to forget that the strongest of compacts bound them not to harm me, that the end of this was fixed by sunset.

Gradually, however, all such rational thoughts blurred in a semidelirium of thirst and pain, narrowing to a red blaze of agony across my shoulder blades. I eased up on my toes again.

White-hot pain blazed through my feet. The rough stone on which my toes sank had been covered with metal and I smelled scorching flesh, jerking up my feet with a wordless snarl of rage and fury, hanging in agony by my shoulders alone.

And then I lost consciousness, at least for several moments, for when I became aware again, through the nightmare of pain, my toes were resting lightly and securely on cold stone. The smell of burned flesh remained, and the painful stinging in my toes. Mingled with that smell was a drift of perfume close by.

Dallisa murmured, "I do not wish to break our bargain by damaging your feet. It's only a little touch of fire to keep you from too much security in resting them."

I felt the taste of blood mingle in my mouth with the sour taste of vomit. I felt delirious, lightheaded. After another eternity I wondered if I had really heard Dallisa's lilting croon or whether it was a nightmare born of feverish pain:

Plead with me. A word, only a word and I will release you, strong man, scarred man. Perhaps I shall demand only a little space in your arms. Would not such doom be light upon you? Perhaps I shall set you free to seek Rakhal if only to plague Kyral. A word, only a word from you. A word, only a word from you....

It died into an endlessly echoing whisper. Swaying, blinded, I wondered why I endured. I drew a dry tongue over lips, salty and bloody, and nightmarishly considered yielding, winning my way somehow around Dallisa. Or knocking her suddenly senseless and escaping—I, who need not be bound by Wolf's codes either. I fumbled with a stiff shape of words.

And a breath saved me, a soft, released breath of anticipation. It was another trick. I swayed, limp and racked. I was not Race Cargill now. I was a dead man hanging in chains, swinging, filthy vultures pecking at my dangling feet. I was....

The sound of boots rang on the stone and Kyral's voice, low and bitter, demanded somewhere behind me, "What have you done with him?"

She did not answer, but I heard her chains clash lightly and imagined her gesture. Kyral muttered, "Women have no genius at any torture except...." His voice faded out into great distances. Their words came to me over a sort of windy ringing, like the howling of lost men, dying in the snowfast passes of the mountains.

"Speak up, you fool, he can't hear you now."

"If you have let him faint, you are clumsy!"

"You talk of clumsiness!" Dallisa's voice, even thinned by the nightmare ringing in my head, held concentrated scorn. "Perhaps I shall release him, to find Rakhal when you failed! The Terrans have a price on Rakhal's head, too. And at least this man will not confuse himself with his prey!"

"If you think I would let you bargain with a Terranan—"

Dallisa cried passionately, "You trade with the Terrans! How would you stop me, then?"

"I trade with them because I must. But for a matter involving the honor of the Great House—"

"The Great House whose steps you would never have climbed, except for Rakhal!" Dallisa sounded as if she were chewing her words in little pieces and spitting them at Kyral. "Oh, you were clever to take us both as your consorts! You did not know it was Rakhal's doing, did you? Hate the Terrans, then!"

She spat an obscenity at him. "Enjoy your hate, wallow in hating, and in the end all Shainsa will fall prey to the Toymaker, like Miellyn."

"If you speak that name again," said Kyral very low, "I will kill you."

"Like Miellyn, Miellyn, Miellyn," Dallisa repeated deliberately. "You fool, Rakhal knew nothing of Miellyn!"

"He was seen—"

"With me, you fool! With me! You cannot yet tell twin from twin? Rakhal came to me to ask news of her!"

Kyral cried out hoarsely, like a man in anguish, "Why didn't you tell me?"

"You don't really have to ask, do you, Kyral?"

"You bitch!" said Kyral. "You filthy bitch!" I heard the sound of a blow. The next moment Kyral ripped the blindfold from my eyes and I blinked in the blaze of light. My arms were wholly numb now, twisted above my head, but the jar of his touch sent fresh pain racing through me. Kyral's face swam out of the blaze of hell. "If that is true, then this is a damnable farce, Dallisa. You have lost our chance of learning what he knows of Miellyn."

"What he knows?" Dallisa lowered her hand from her face, where a bruise was already darkening.

"Miellyn has twice appeared when I was with him. Loose him, Dallisa, and bargain with him. What we know of Rakhal for what he knows of Miellyn."

"If you think I would let you bargain with Terranan," she mocked. "Weakling, this quarrel is mine! You fool, the others in the caravan will give me news, if you will not! Where is Cuinn?"

From a million miles away Kyral laughed. "You've slipped the wrong hawk, Dallisa. The catmen killed him." His skean flicked loose. He climbed to a perch near the rope at my wrists. "Bargain with me, Rascar!"

I coughed, unable to speak, and Kyral insisted, "Will you bargain? End this damned woman's farce which makes a mock of shegri?"

The slant of sun told me there was light left. I found a shred of voice, not knowing what I was going to say until I had said it, irrevocably. "This is between Dallisa and me."

Kyral glared at me in mounting rage. With four strides he was out of the room, flinging back a harsh, furious "I hope you kill each other!" and the door slammed.

Dallisa's face swam red, and again as before, I knew the battle which was joined between us would be fought to a dreadful end. She touched my chest lightly, but the touch jolted excruciating pain through my shoulders.

"Did you kill Cuinn?"

I wondered, wearily, what this presaged.

"Did you?" In a passion, she cried, "Answer! Did you kill him?" She struck me hard, and where the touch had been pain, the blow was a blaze of white agony. I fainted.

"Answer!" She struck me again and the white blaze jolted me back to consciousness. "Answer me! Answer!" Each cry bought a blow until I gasped finally, "He signaled ... set catmen on us...."

"No!" She stood staring at me and her white face was a death mask in which the eyes lived. She screamed wildly and the huge chak came running.

"Cut him down! Cut him down! Cut him down!"

A knife slashed the rope and I slumped, falling in a bone-breaking huddle to the floor. My arms were still twisted over my head. The chak cut the ropes apart, pulled my arms roughly back into place, and I gagged with the pain as the blood began flowing painfully through the chafed and swollen hands.

And then I lost consciousness. More or less permanently, this time.

Chapter Nine

When I came to again I was lying with my head in Dallisa's lap, and the reddish color of sunset was in the room. Her thighs were soft under my head, and for an instant I wondered if, in delirium, I had conceded to her. I muttered, "Sun ... not down...."

She bent her face to mine, whispering, "Hush. Hush."

It was heaven, and I drifted off again. After a moment I felt a cup against my lips.

"Can you swallow this?"

I could and did. I couldn't taste it yet, but it was cold and wet and felt heavenly trickling down my throat. She bent and looked into my eyes, and I felt as if I were falling into those reddish and stormy depths. She touched my scarred mouth with a light finger. Suddenly my head cleared and I sat upright.

"Is this a trick to force me into calling my bet?"

She recoiled as if I had struck her, then the trace of a smile flitted around her red mouth. Yes, between us it was battle. "You are right to be suspicious, I suppose. But if I tell you what I know of Rakhal, will you trust me then?"

I looked straight at her and said, "No."

Surprisingly, she threw back her head and laughed. I flexed my freed wrists cautiously. The skin was torn away and chafed, and my arms ached to the bone. When I moved harsh lances of pain drove through my chest.

"Well, until sunset I have no right to ask you to trust me," said Dallisa when she had done laughing. "And since you are bound by my command until the last ray has fallen, I command that you lay your head upon my knees."

I blazed, "You are making a game of me!"

"Is that my privilege? Do you refuse?"

"Refuse?" It was not yet sunset. This might be a torture more complex than any which had yet greeted me. From the scarlet glint in her eyes I felt she was playing with me, as the cat-things of the forest play with their helpless victims. My mouth twitched in a grimace of humiliation as I lowered myself obediently until my head rested on her fur-clad knees.

She murmured, smiling, "Is this so unbearable, then?"

I said nothing. Never, never for an instant could I forget that—all human, all woman as she seemed—Dallisa's race was worn and old when the Terran Empire had not left their home star. The mind of Wolf, which has mingled with the nonhuman since before the beginnings of recorded time, is unfathomable to an outsider. I was better equipped than most Earthmen to keep pace with its surface acts, but I could never pretend to understand its deeper motivations.

It works on complex and irrational logic. Mischief is an integral part of it. Even the deadly blood-feud with Rakhal had begun with an overelaborate practical joke—which had lost the Service, incidentally, several thousand credits worth of spaceship.

And so I could not trust Dallisa for an instant. Yet it was wonderful to lie here with my head resting against the perfumed softness of her body.

Then suddenly her arms were gripping me, frantic and hungry; the subdued thing in her voice, her eyes, flamed out hot and wild. She was pressing the whole length of her body to mine, breasts and thighs and long legs, and her voice was hoarse.

"Is this torture too?"

Beneath the fur robe she was soft and white, and the subtle scent of her hair seemed a deeper entrapment than any. Frail as she seemed, her arms had the strength of steel, and pain blazed down my wrenched shoulders, seared through the twisted wrists. Then I forgot the pain.

Over her shoulder the last dropping redness of the sun vanished and plunged the room into orchid twilight.

I caught her wrists in my hands, prizing them backward, twisting them upward over her head. I said thickly, "The sun's down." And then I stopped her wild mouth with mine.

And I knew that the battle between us had reached climax and victory simultaneously, and any question about who had won it was purely academic.

During the night sometime, while her dark head lay motionless on my shoulder, I found myself staring into the darkness, wakeful. The throbbing of my bruises had little to do with my sleeplessness; I was remembering other chained girls from the old days in the Dry-towns, and the honey and poison of them distilled into Dallisa's kisses. Her head was very light on my shoulders, and she felt curiously insubstantial, like a woman of feathers.

One of the tiny moons was visible through the slitted windows. I thought of my rooms in the Terran Trade City, clean and bright and warm, and all the nights when I had paced the floor, hating, filled to the teeth with bitterness, longing for the windswept stars of the Dry-towns, the salt smell of the winds and the musical clashing of the walk of the chained women.

With a sting of guilt, I realized that I had half forgotten Juli and my pledge to her and her misfortune which had freed me again, for this.

Yet I had won, and what they knew had narrowed my planet-wide search to a pinpoint. Rakhal was in Charin.

I wasn't altogether surprised. Charin is the only city on Wolf, except the Kharsa, where the Terran Empire has put down deep roots into the planet, built a Trade City, a smaller spaceport. Like the Kharsa, it lies within the circle of Terran law—and a million miles outside it.

A nonhuman town, inhabited largely by chaks, it is the core and center of the resistance movement, a noisy town in a perpetual ferment. It was the logical place for a renegade. I settled myself so that the ache in my racked shoulders was less violent, and muttered, "Why Charin?"

Slight as the movement was, it roused Dallisa. She rolled over and propped herself on her elbows, quoting drowsily, "The prey walks safest at the hunter's door."

I stared at the square of violet moonlight, trying to fit together all the pieces of the puzzle, and asked half aloud, "What prey and what hunters?"

Dallisa didn't answer. I hadn't expected her to answer. I asked the real question in my mind: "Why does Kyral hate Rakhal Sensar, when he doesn't even know him by sight?"

"There are reasons," she said somberly. "One of them is Miellyn, my twin sister. Kyral climbed the steps of the Great House by claiming us both as his consorts. He is our father's son by another wife."

That explained much. Brother-and-sister marriages, not uncommon in the Dry-towns, are based on expediency and suspicion, and are frequently, though not always loveless. It explained Dallisa's taunts, and it partly explained, only partly, why I found her in my arms. It did not explain Rakhal's part in this mysterious intrigue, nor why Kyral had taken me for Rakhal, (but only after he remembered seeing me in Terran clothing).

I wondered why it had never occurred to me before that I might be mistaken for Rakhal. There was no close resemblance between us, but a casual description would apply equally well to me or to Rakhal. My height is unusual for a Terran—within an inch of Rakhal's own—and we had roughly the same build, the same coloring. I had copied his walk, imitated his mannerisms, since we were boys together.

And, blurring minor facial characteristics, there were the scars of the kifirgh on my mouth, cheeks, and shoulders. Anyone who did not know us by sight, anyone who had known us by reputation from the days when we had worked together in the Dry-towns, might easily take one of us for the other. Even Juli had blurted, "You're so much like—" before thinking better of it.

Other odd bits of the puzzle floated in my mind, stubbornly refusing to take on recognizable patterns, the disappearance of a toy-seller; Juli's hysterical babbling; the way the girl—Miellyn?—had vanished into a shrine of Nebran; and the taunts of Dallisa and the old man about a mysterious "Toymaker." And something, some random joggling of a memory, in that eerie trading in the city of the Silent Ones. I knew all these things fitted together somehow, but I had no real hope that Dallisa could complete their pattern for me.

She said, with a vehemence that startled me, "Miellyn is only the excuse! Kyral hates Rakhal because Rakhal will compromise and because he'll fight!"

She rolled over and pressed herself against me in the darkness. Her voice trembled. "Race, our world is dying. We can't stand against Terra. And there are other things, worse things."

I sat up, surprised to find myself defending Terra to this girl. After all these years I was back in my own world. And yet I heard myself say quietly, "The Terrans aren't exploiting Wolf. We haven't abolished the rule of Shainsa. We've changed nothing."

It was true. Terra held Wolf by compact, not conquest. They paid, and paid generously, for the lease of the lands where their Trade Cities would rise, and stepped beyond them only when invited to do so.

"We let any city or state that wants to keep its independence govern itself until it collapses, Dallisa. And they do collapse after a generation or so. Very few primitive planets can hold out against us. The people themselves get tired of living under feudal or theocratic systems, and they beg to be taken into the Empire. That's all."

"But that's just it," Dallisa argued. "You give the people all those things we used to give them, and you do it better. Just by being here, you are killing the Dry-towns. They're turning to you and leaving us, and you let them do it."

I shook my head. "We've kept the Terran Peace for centuries. What do you expect? Should we give you arms, planes, bombs, weapons to hold your slaves down?"

"Yes!" she flared at me. "The Dry-towns have ruled Wolf since—since—you, you can't even imagine how long! And we made compact with you to trade here—"

"And we have rewarded you by leaving you untouched," I said quietly. "But we have not forbidden the Dry-towns to come into the Empire and work with Terra."

She said bitterly, "Men like Kyral will die first," and pressed her face helplessly against me. "And I will die with them. Miellyn broke away, but I cannot! Courage is what I lack. Our world is rotten, Race, rotten all through, and I'm as rotten as the core of it. I could have killed you today, and I'm here in your arms. Our world is rotten, but I've no confidence that the new world will be better!"

I put my hand under her chin, and looked down gravely into her face, only a pale oval in the darkness. There was nothing I could say; she had said it all, and truthfully. I had hated and yearned and starved for this, and when I found it, it turned salty and bloody on my lips, like Dallisa's despairing kisses. She ran her fingers over the scars on my face, then gripped her small thin hands around my wrists so fiercely that I grunted protest.

"You will not forget me," she said in her strangely lilting voice. "You will not forget me, although you were victorious." She twisted and lay looking up at me, her eyes glowing faintly luminous in darkness. I knew that she could see me as clearly as if it were day. "I think it was my victory, not yours, Race Cargill."

Gently, on an impulse I could not explain, I picked up one delicate wrist, then the other, unclasping the heavy jeweled bracelets. She let out a stifled cry of dismay. And then I tossed the chains into a corner before I drew her savagely into my arms again and forced her head back under my mouth.

I said good-bye to her alone, in the reddish, windswept space before the Great House. She pressed her head against my shoulder and whispered, "Race, take me with you!"

For answer I only picked up her narrow wrists and turned them over on my palm. The jeweled bracelets were clasped again around the thinly boned joints, and on some self-punishing impulse she had shortened the chains so that she could not even put her arms around me. I lifted the punished wrists to my mouth and kissed them gently.

"You don't want to leave, Dallisa."

I was desperately sorry for her. She would go down with her dying world, proud and cold and with no place in the new one. She kissed me and I tasted blood, her thin fettered body straining wildly against me, shaken with tearing, convulsive sobs. Then she turned and fled back into the shadow of the great dark house.

I never saw her again.

Chapter Ten

A few days later I found myself nearing the end of the trail.

It was twilight in Charin, hot and reeking with the gypsy glare of fires which burned, smoking, at the far end of the Street of the Six Shepherds. I crouched in the shadow of a wall, waiting.

My skin itched from the dirty shirtcloak I hadn't changed in days. Shabbiness is wise in nonhuman parts, and Dry-towners think too much of water to waste much of it in superfluous washing anyhow. I scratched unobtrusively and glanced cautiously down the street.

It seemed empty, except for a few sodden derelicts sprawled in doorways—the Street of the Six Shepherds is a filthy slum—but I made sure my skean was loose. Charin is not a particularly safe town, even for Dry-towners, and especially not for Earthmen, at any time.

Even with what Dallisa had told me, the search had been difficult. Charin is not Shainsa. In Charin, where human and nonhuman live closer together than anywhere else on the planet, information about such men as Rakhal can be bought, but the policy is to let the buyer beware. That's fair enough, because the life of the seller has a way of not being worth much afterward, either.

A dirty, dust-laden wind was blowing up along the street, heavy with strange smells. The pungent reek of incense from a street-shrine was in the smells. The heavy, acrid odor that made my skin crawl. In the hills behind Charin, the Ghost Wind was rising.

Borne on this wind, the Ya-men would sweep down from the mountains, and everything human or nearly human would scatter in their path. They would range through the quarter all night, and in the morning they would melt away, until the Ghost Wind blew again. At any other time, I would already have taken cover. I fancied that I could hear, borne on the wind, the faraway yelping, and envision the plumed, taloned figures which would come leaping down the street.

In that moment, the quiet of the street split asunder.

From somewhere a girl's voice screamed in shrill pain or panic. Then I saw her, dodging between two of the chinked pebble-houses. She was a child, thin and barefoot, a long tangle of black hair flying loose as she darted and twisted to elude the lumbering fellow at her heels. His outstretched paw jerked cruelly at her slim wrist.

The little girl screamed and wrenched herself free and threw herself straight on me, wrapping herself around my neck with the violence of a storm wind. Her hair got in my mouth and her small hands gripped at my back like a cat's flexed claws.

"Oh, help me," she gasped between sobs. "Don't let him get me, don't." And even in that broken plea I took it in that the little ragamuffin did not speak the jargon of that slum, but the pure speech of Shainsa.

What I did then was as automatic as if it had been Juli. I pulled the kid loose, shoved her behind me, and scowled at the brute who lurched toward us.

"Make yourself scarce," I advised. "We don't chase little girls where I come from. Haul off, now."

The man reeled. I smelled the rankness of his rags as he thrust one grimy paw at the girl. I never was the hero type, but I'd started something which I had to carry through. I thrust myself between them and put my hand on the skean again.

"You—you Dry-towner." The man set up a tipsy howl, and I sucked in my breath. Now I was in for it. Unless I got out of there damned fast, I'd lose what I'd come all the way to Charin to find.

I felt like handing the girl over. For all I knew, the bully could be her father and she was properly in line for a spanking. This wasn't any of my business. My business lay at the end of the street, where Rakhal was waiting at the fires. He wouldn't be there long. Already the smell of the Ghost Wind was heavy and harsh, and little flurries of sand went racing along the street, lifting the flaps of the doorways.

But I did nothing so sensible. The big lunk made a grab at the girl, and I whipped out my skean and pantomimed.

"Get going!"

"Dry-towner!" He spat out the word like filth, his pig-eyes narrowing to slits. "Son of the Ape! Earthman!"

"Terranan!" Someone took up the howl. There was a stir, a rustle, all along the street that had seemed empty, and from nowhere, it seemed, the space in front of me was crowded with shadowy forms, human and otherwise.

"Earthman!"

I felt the muscles across my belly knotting into a band of ice. I didn't believe I'd given myself away as an Earthman. The bully was using the time-dishonored tactic of stirring up a riot in a hurry, but just the same I looked quickly round, hunting a path of escape.

"Put your skean in his guts, Spilkar! Grab him!"

"Hai-ai! Earthman! Hai-ai!"

It was the last cry that made me panic. Through the sultry glare at the end of the street, I could see the plumed, taloned figures of the Ya-men, gliding through the banners of smoke. The crowd melted open.

I didn't stop to reflect on the fact—suddenly very obvious—that Rakhal couldn't have been at the fires at all, and that my informant had led me into an open trap, a nest of Ya-men already inside Charin. The crowd edged back and muttered, and suddenly I made my choice. I whirled, snatched up the girl in my arms and ran straight toward the advancing figures of the Ya-men.

Nobody followed me. I even heard a choked shout that sounded like a warning. I heard the yelping shrieks of the Ya-men grow to a wild howl, and at the last minute, when their stiff rustling plumes loomed only a few yards away, I dived sidewise into an alley, stumbled on some rubbish and spilled the girl down.

"Run, kid!"

She shook herself like a puppy climbing out of water. Her small fingers closed like a steel trap on my wrist. "This way," she urged in a hasty whisper, and I found myself plunging out the far end of the alley and into the shelter of a street-shrine. The sour stink of incense smarted in my nostrils, and I could hear the yelping of the Ya-men as they leaped and rustled down the alley, their cold and poisonous eyes searching out the recess where I crouched with the girl.

"Here," she panted, "stand close to me on the stone—" I drew back, startled.

"Oh, don't stop to argue," she whimpered. "Come here!"

"Hai-ai! Earthman! There he is!"

The girl's arms flung round me again. I felt her slight, hard body pressing on mine and she literally hauled me toward the pattern of stones at the center of the shrine. I wouldn't have been human if I hadn't caught her closer yet.

The world reeled. The street disappeared in a cone of spinning lights, stars danced crazily, and I plunged down through a widening gulf of empty space, locked in the girl's arms. I fell, spun, plunged head over heels through tilting lights and shadows that flung us through eternities of freefall. The yelping of the Ya-men whirled away in unimaginable distances, and for a second I felt the unmerciful blackout of a power dive, with blood breaking from my nostrils and filling my mouth.

Chapter Eleven

Lights flared in my eyes.

I was standing solidly on my feet in the street-shrine, but the street was gone. Coils of incense still smudged the air. The God squatted toadlike in his recess. The girl was hanging limp, locked in my clenched arms. As the floor straightened under my feet I staggered, thrown off balance by the sudden return of the girl's weight, and grabbed blindly for support.

"Give her to me," said a voice, and the girl's sagging body was lifted from my arms. A strong hand grasped my elbow. I found a chair beneath my knees and sank gratefully into it.

"The transmission isn't smooth yet between such distant terminals," the voice remarked. "I see Miellyn has fainted again. A weakling, the girl, but useful."

I spat blood, trying to get the room in focus. For I was inside a room, a room of some translucent substance, windowless, a skylight high above me, through which pink daylight streamed. Daylight—and it had been midnight in Charin! I'd come halfway around the planet in a few seconds!

From somewhere I heard the sound of hammering, tiny, bell-like hammering, the chiming of a fairy anvil. I looked up and saw a man—a man?—watching me.

On Wolf you see all kinds of human, half-human and nonhuman life, and I consider myself something of an expert on all three. But I had never seen anyone, or anything, who so closely resembled the human and so obviously wasn't. He, or it, was tall and lean, man-shaped but oddly muscled, a vague suggestion of something less than human in the lean hunch of his posture.

Manlike, he wore green tight-fitting trunks and a shirt of green fur that revealed bulging biceps where they shouldn't be, and angular planes where there should have been swelling muscles. The shoulders were high, the neck unpleasantly sinuous, and the face, a little narrower than human, was handsomely arrogant, with a kind of wary alert mischief that was the least human thing about him.

He bent, tilted the girl's inert body on to a divan of some sort, and turned his back on her, lifting his hand in an impatient, and unpleasantly reminiscent, gesture.

The tinkling of the little hammers stopped as if a switch had been disconnected.

"Now," said the nonhuman, "we can talk."

Like the waif, he spoke Shainsan, and spoke it with a better accent than any nonhuman I had ever known—so well that I looked again to be certain. I wasn't too dazed to answer in the same tongue, but I couldn't keep back a spate of questions:

"What happened? Who are you? What is this place?"

The nonhuman waited, crossing his hands—quite passable hands, if you didn't look too closely at what should have been nails—and bent forward in a sketchy gesture.

"Do not blame Miellyn. She acted under orders. It was imperative you be brought here tonight, and we had reason to believe you might ignore an ordinary summons. You were clever at evading our surveillance, for a time. But there would not be two Dry-towners in Charin tonight who would dare the Ghost Wind. Your reputation does you justice, Rakhal Sensar."

Rakhal Sensar! Once again Rakhal!

Shaken, I pulled a rag from my pocket and wiped blood from my mouth. I'd figured out, in Shainsa, why the mistake was logical. And here in Charin I'd been hanging around in Rakhal's old haunts, covering his old trails. Once again, mistaken identity was natural.

Natural or not, I wasn't going to deny it. If these were Rakhal's enemies, my real identity should be kept as an ace in reserve which might—just might—get me out alive again. If they were his friends ... well, I could only hope that no one who knew him well by sight would walk in on me.

"We knew," the nonhuman continued, "that if you remained where you were, the Terranan Cargill would have made his arrest. We know about your quarrel with Cargill, among other things, but we did not consider it necessary that you should fall into his hands at present."

I was puzzled. "I still don't understand. Exactly where am I?"

"This is the mastershrine of Nebran."

Nebran!

The stray pieces of the puzzle suddenly jolted into place. Kyral had warned me, not knowing he was doing it. I hastily imitated the gesture Kyral had made, gabbling a few words of an archaic charm.

Like every Earthman who's lived on Wolf more than a tourist season, I'd seen faces go blank and impassive at mention of the Toad God. Rumor made his spies omnipresent, his priests omniscient, his anger all-powerful. I had believed about a tenth of what I had heard, or less.

The Terran Empire has little to say to planetary religions, and Nebran's cult is a remarkably obscure one, despite the street-shrines on every corner. Now I was in his mastershrine, and the device which had brought me here was beyond doubt a working model of a matter transmitter.

A matter transmitter, a working model—the words triggered memory. Rakhal was after it.

"And who," I asked slowly, "are you, Lord?"

The green-clad creature hunched thin shoulders again in a ceremonious gesture. "I am called Evarin. Humble servant of Nebran and yourself," he added, but there was no humility in his manner. "I am called the Toymaker."

Evarin. That was another name given weight by rumor. A breath of gossip in a thieves market. A scrawled word on smudged paper. A blank folder in Terran Intelligence. Another puzzle-piece snapped into place—Toymaker!

The girl on the divan sat up suddenly passing slim hands over her disheveled hair. "Did I faint, Evarin? I had to fight to get him into the stone, and the patterns were not set straight in that terminal. You must send one of the Little Ones to set them to rights. Toymaker, you are not listening to me."

"Stop chattering, Miellyn," said Evarin indifferently. "You brought him here, and that is all that matters. You aren't hurt?"

Miellyn pouted and looked ruefully at her bare bruised feet, patted the wrinkles in her ragged frock with fastidious fingers. "My poor feet," she mourned, "they are black and blue with the cobbles and my hair is filled with sand and tangles! Toymaker, what way was this to send me to entice a man? Any man would have come quickly, quickly, if he had seen me looking lovely, but you—you send me in rags!"

She stamped a small bare foot. She was not merely as young as she had looked in the street. Though immature and underdeveloped by Terran standards, she had a fair figure for a Dry-town woman. Her rags fell now in graceful folds. Her hair was spun black glass, and I—I saw what the rags and the confusion in the filthy street had kept me from seeing before.

It was the girl of the spaceport cafe, the girl who had appeared and vanished in the eerie streets of Canarsa.

Evarin was regarding her with what, in a human, might have been rueful impatience. He said, "You know you enjoyed yourself, as always, Miellyn. Run along and make yourself beautiful again, little nuisance."

The girl danced out of the room, and I was just as glad to see her go. The Toymaker motioned to me.

"This way," he directed, and led me through a different door. The offstage hammering I had heard, tiny bell tones like a fairy xylophone, began again as the door opened, and we passed into a workroom which made me remember nursery tales from a half-forgotten childhood on Terra. For the workers were tiny, gnarled trolls!

They were chaks. Chaks from the polar mountains, dwarfed and furred and half-human, with witchlike faces and great golden eyes, and I had the curious feeling that if I looked hard enough I would see the little toy-seller they had hunted out of the Kharsa. I didn't look. I figured I was in enough trouble already.

Tiny hammers pattered on miniature anvils in a tinkling, jingling chorus of musical clinks and taps. Golden eyes focused like lenses over winking jewels and gimcracks. Busy elves. Makers of toys!

Evarin jerked his shoulders with an imperative gesture. I followed him through a fairy workroom, but could not refrain from casting a lingering look at the worktables. A withered leprechaun set eyes into the head of a minikin hound. Furred fingers worked precious metals into invisible filigree for the collarpiece of a dancing doll. Metallic feathers were thrust with clockwork precision into the wings of a skeleton bird no longer than my fingernail. The nose of the hound wabbled and sniffed, the bird's wings quivered, the eyes of the little dancer followed my footsteps.

Toys?

"This way," Evarin rapped, and a door slid shut behind us. The clinks and taps grew faint, fainter, but never ceased.

My face must have betrayed more than conventional impassivity, for Evarin smiled. "Now you know, Rakhal, why I am called Toymaker. Is it not strange—the masterpriest of Nebran, a maker of Toys, and the shrine of the Toad God a workshop for children's playthings?"

Evarin paused suggestively. They were obviously not children's playthings and this was my cue to say so, but I avoided the trap. Evarin opened a sliding panel and took out a doll.

She was perhaps the length of my longest finger, molded to the precise proportions of a woman, and costumed after the bizarre fashion of the Ardcarran dancing girls. Evarin touched no button or key that I could see, but when he set the figure on its feet, it executed a whirling, armtossing dance in a fast, tricky tempo.

"I am, in a sense, benevolent," Evarin murmured. He snapped his fingers and the doll sank to her knees and poised there, silent. "Moreover, I have the means and, let us say, the ability to indulge my small fantasies.

"The little daughter of the President of the Federation of Trade Cities on Samarra was sent such a doll recently. What a pity that Paolo Arimengo was so suddenly impeached and banished!" The Toymaker clucked his teeth commiseratingly. "Perhaps this small companion will compensate the little Carmela for her adjustment to her new ... position."

He replaced the dancer and pulled down something like a whirligig. "This might interest you," he mused, and set it spinning. I stared at the pattern of lights that flowed and disappeared, melting in and out of visible shadows. Suddenly I realized what the thing was doing. I wrested my eyes away with an effort. Had there been a lapse of seconds or minutes? Had Evarin spoken?

Evarin arrested the compelling motion with one finger. "Several of these pretty playthings are available to the children of important men," he said absently. "An import of value for our exploited and impoverished world. Unfortunately they are, perhaps, a little ... ah, obvious. The incidence of nervous breakdowns is, ah, interfering with their sale. The children, of course, are unaffected, and love them." Evarin set the hypnotic wheel moving again, glanced sidewise at me, then set it carefully back.

"Now"—Evarin's voice, hard with the silkiness of a cat's snarl, clawed the silence—"we'll talk business."

I turned, composing my face. Evarin had something concealed in one hand, but I didn't think it was a weapon. And if I'd known, I'd have had to ignore it anyway.

"Perhaps you wonder how we recognized and found you?" A panel cleared in the wall and became translucent. Confused flickers moved, dropped into focus and I realized that the panel was an ordinary television screen and I was looking into the well-known interior of the Cafe of Three Rainbows in the Trade City of Charin.

By this time I was running low on curiosity and didn't wonder till much, much later how televised pictures were transmitted around the curve of a planet. Evarin sharpened the focus down on the long Earth-type bar where a tall man in Terran clothes was talking to a pale-haired girl. Evarin said, "By now, Race Cargill has decided, no doubt, that you fell into his trap and into the hands of the Ya-men. He is off-guard now."

And suddenly the whole thing seemed so unbearably, illogically funny that my shoulders shook with the effort to keep back dangerous laughter. Since I'd landed in Charin, I'd taken great pains to avoid the Trade City, or anyone who might have associated me with it. And Rakhal, somehow aware of this, had conveniently filled up the gap. By posing as me.

It wasn't nearly as difficult as it sounded. I had found that out in Shainsa. Charin is a long, long way from the major Trade City near the Kharsa. I hadn't a single intimate friend there, or within hundreds of miles, to see through the imposture. At most, there were half a dozen of the staff that I'd once met, or had a drink with, eight or ten years ago.

Rakhal could speak perfect Standard when he chose; if he lapsed into Dry-town idiom, that too was in my known character. I had no doubt he was making a great success of it all, probably doing much better with my identity than I could ever have done with his.

Evarin rasped, "Cargill meant to leave the planet. What stopped him? You could be of use to us, Rakhal. But not with this blood-feud unsettled."

That needed no elucidation. No Wolfan in his right mind will bargain with a Dry-towner carrying an unresolved blood-feud. By law and custom, declared blood-feud takes precedence over any other business, public or private, and is sufficient excuse for broken promises, neglected duties, theft, even murder.

"We want it settled once and for all." Evarin's voice was low and unhurried. "And we aren't above weighting the scales. This Cargill can, and has, posed as a Dry-towner, undetected. We don't like Earthmen who can do that. In settling your feud, you will be aiding us, and removing a danger. We would be ... grateful."

He opened his closed hand, displaying something small, curled, inert.

"Every living thing emits a characteristic pattern of electrical nerve impulses. We have ways of recording those impulses, and we have had you and Cargill under observation for a long time. We've had plenty of opportunity to key this Toy to Cargill's pattern."

On his palm the curled thing stirred, spread wings. A fledgling bird lay there, small soft body throbbing slightly. Half-hidden in a ruff of metallic feathers I glimpsed a grimly elongated beak. The pinions were feathered with delicate down less than a quarter of an inch long. They beat with delicate insistence against the Toymaker's prisoning fingers.

"This is not dangerous to you. Press here"—he showed me—"and if Race Cargill is within a certain distance—and it is up to you to be within that distance—it will find him, and kill him. Unerringly, inescapably, untraceably. We will not tell you the critical distance. And we will give you three days."

He checked my startled exclamation with a gesture. "Of course this is a test. Within the hour Cargill will receive a warning. We want no incompetents who must be helped too much! Nor do we want cowards! If you fail, or release the bird at a distance too great, or evade the test"—the green inhuman malice in his eyes made me sweat—"we have made another bird."

By now my brain was swimming, but I thought I understood the complex inhuman logic involved. "The other bird is keyed to me?"

With slow contempt Evarin shook his head. "You? You are used to danger and fond of a gamble. Nothing so simple! We have given you three days. If, within that time, the bird you carry has not killed, the other bird will fly. And it will kill. Rakhal, you have a wife."

Yes, Rakhal had a wife. They could threaten Rakhal's wife. And his wife was my sister Juli.

Everything after that was anticlimax. Of course I had to drink with Evarin, the elaborate formal ritual without which no bargain on Wolf is concluded. He entertained me with gory and technical descriptions of the way in which the birds, and other of his hellish Toys, did their killing, and worse tasks.

Miellyn danced into the room and upset the exquisite solemnity of the wine-ritual by perching on my knee, stealing a sip from my cup, and pouting prettily when I paid her less attention than she thought she merited. I didn't dare pay much attention, even when she whispered, with the deliberate and thorough wantonness of a Dry-town woman of high-caste who has flung aside her fetters, something about a rendezvous at the Three Rainbows.

But eventually it was over and I stepped through a door that twisted with a giddy blankness, and found myself outside a bare windowless wall in Charin again, the night sky starred and cold. The acrid smell of the Ghost Wind was thinning in the streets, but I had to crouch in a cranny of the wall when a final rustling horde of Ya-men, the last of their receding tide, rustled down the street. I found my way to my lodging in a filthy chak hostel, and threw myself down on the verminous bed.

Believe it or not, I slept.

Chapter Twelve

An hour before dawn there was a noise in my room. I roused, my hand on my skean. Someone or something was fumbling under the mattress where I had thrust Evarin's bird. I struck out, encountered something warm and breathing, and grappled with it in the darkness. A foul-smelling something gripped over my mouth. I tore it away and struck hard with the skean. There was a high shrilling. The gripping filth loosened and fell away and something died on the floor.

I struck a light, retching in revulsion. It hadn't been human. There wouldn't have been that much blood from a human. Not that color, either.

The chak who ran the place came and gibbered at me. Chaks have a horror of blood and this one gave me to understand that my lease was up then and there, no arguments, no refunds. He wouldn't even let me go into his stone outbuilding to wash the foul stuff from my shirtcloak. I gave up and fished under the mattress for Evarin's Toy.

The chak got a glimpse of the embroideries on the silk in which it was wrapped, and stood back, his loose furry lips hanging open, while I gathered my few belongings together and strode out of the room. He would not touch the coins I offered; I laid them on a chest and he let them lie there, and as I went into the reddening morning they came flying after me into the street.

I pulled the silk from the Toy and tried to make some sense from my predicament. The little thing lay innocent and silent in my palm. It wouldn't tell me whether it had been keyed to me, the real Cargill, some time in the past, or to Rakhal, using my name and reputation in the Terran Colony here at Charin.

If I pressed the stud it might play out this comedy of errors by hunting down Rakhal, and all my troubles would be over. For a while, at least, until Evarin found out what had happened. I didn't deceive myself that I could carry the impersonation through another meeting.

On the other hand, if I pressed the stud, the bird might turn on me. And then all my troubles would be over for good.

If I delayed past Evarin's deadline, and did nothing, the other bird in his keeping would hunt down Juli and give her a swift and not too painless death.

I spent most of the day in a chak dive, juggling plans. Toys, innocent and sinister. Spies, messengers. Toys which killed horribly. Toys which could be controlled, perhaps, by the pliant mind of a child, and every child hates its parents now and again!

Even in the Terran colony, who was safe? In Mack's very home, one of the Magnusson youngsters had a shiny thing which might, or might not, be one of Evarin's hellish Toys. Or was I beginning to think like a superstitious Dry-towner?

Damn it, Evarin couldn't be infallible; he hadn't even recognized me as Race Cargill! Or—suddenly the sweat broke out, again, on my forehead—or had he? Had the whole thing been one of those sinister, deadly and incomprehensible nonhuman jokes?

I kept coming to the same conclusion. Juli was in danger, but she was half a world away. Rakhal was here in Charin. There was a child involved—Juli's child. The first step was to get inside the Terran colony and see how the land lay.

Charin is a city shaped like a crescent moon, encircling the small Trade City: a miniature spaceport, a miniature skyscraper HQ, the clustered dwellings of the Terrans who worked there, and those who lived with them and supplied them with necessities, services and luxuries.

Entry from one to the other is through a guarded gateway, since this is hostile territory, and Charin lies far beyond the impress of ordinary Terran law. But the gate stood wide-open, and the guards looked lax and bored. They had shockers, but they didn't look as if they'd used them lately.

One raised an eyebrow at his companion as I shambled up. I could pretty well guess the impression I made, dirty, unkempt and stained with nonhuman blood. I asked permission to go into the Terran Zone.

They asked my name and business, and I toyed with the notion of giving the name of the man I was inadvertently impersonating. Then I decided that if Rakhal had passed himself off as Race Cargill, he'd expect exactly that. And he was also capable of the masterstroke of impudence—putting out a pickup order, through Spaceforce, for his own name!

So I gave the name we'd used from Shainsa to Charin, and tacked one of the Secret Service passwords on the end of it. They looked at each other again and one said, "Rascar, eh? This is the guy, all right." He took me into the little booth by the gate while the other used an intercom device. Presently they took me along into the HQ building, and into an office that said "Legate."

I tried not to panic, but it wasn't easy! Evidently I'd walked square into another trap. One guard asked me, "All right, now, what exactly is your business in the Trade City?"

I'd hoped to locate Rakhal first. Now I knew I'd have no chance and at all costs I must straighten out this matter of identity before it went any further.

"Put me straight through to Magnusson's office, Level 38 at Central HQ, by visi," I demanded. I was trying to remember if Mack had ever even heard the name we used in Shainsa. I decided I couldn't risk it. "Name of Race Cargill."

The guard grinned without moving. He said to his partner, "That's the one, all right." He put a hand on my shoulder, spinning me around.

"Haul off, man. Shake your boots."

There were two of them, and Spaceforce guards aren't picked for their good looks. Just the same, I gave a pretty good account of myself until the inner door opened and a man came storming out.

"What the devil is all this racket?"

One guard got a hammerlock on me. "This Dry-towner bum tried to talk us into making a priority call to Magnusson, the Chief at Central. He knew a couple of the S.S. passwords. That's what got him through the gate. Remember, Cargill passed the word that somebody would turn up trying to impersonate him."

"I remember." The strange man's eyes were wary and cold.

"You damned fools," I snarled. "Magnusson will identify me! Can't you realize you're dealing with an impostor?"

One of the guards said to the legate in an undertone, "Maybe we ought to hold him as a suspicious character." But the legate shook his head. "Not worth the trouble. Cargill said it was a private affair. You might search him, make sure he's not concealing contraband weapons," he added, and talked softly to the wide-eyed clerk in the background while the guards went through my shirtcloak and pockets.

When they started to unwrap the silk-shrouded Toy I yelled—if the thing got set off accidentally, there'd be trouble. The legate turned and rebuked, "Can't you see it's embroidered with the Toad God? It's a religious amulet of some sort, let it alone."

They grumbled, but gave it back to me, and the legate commanded, "Don't mess him up any more. Give him back his knife and take him to the gates. But make sure he doesn't come back."

I found myself seized and frog-marched to the gate. One guard pushed my skean back into its clasp. The other shoved me hard, and I stumbled, fell sprawling in the dust of the cobbled street, to the accompaniment of a profane statement about what I could expect if I came back. A chorus of jeers from a cluster of chak children and veiled women broke across me.

I picked myself up, glowered so fiercely at the giggling spectators that the laughter drained away into silence, and clenched my fists, half inclined to turn back and bull my way through. Then I subsided. First round to Rakhal. He had sprung the trap on me, very neatly.

The street was narrow and crooked, winding between doubled rows of pebble-houses, and full of dark shadows even in the crimson noon. I walked aimlessly, favoring the arm the guard had crushed. I was no closer to settling things with Rakhal, and I had slammed at least one gate behind me.

Why hadn't I had sense enough to walk up and demand to see Race Cargill? Why hadn't I insisted on a fingerprint check? I could prove my identity, and Rakhal, using my name in my absence, to those who didn't know me by sight, couldn't. I could at least have made him try. But he had maneuvered it very cleverly, so I never had a chance to insist on proofs.

I turned into a wineshop and ordered a dram of greenish mountainberry liquor, sipping it slowly and fingering the few bills and coins in my pockets. I'd better forget about warning Juli. I couldn't 'vise her from Charin, except in the Terran zone. I had neither the money nor the time to make the trip in person, even if I could get passage on a Terran-dominated airline after today.

Miellyn. She had flirted with me, and like Dallisa, she might prove vulnerable. It might be another trap, but I'd take the chance. At least I could get hints about Evarin. And I needed information. I wasn't used to this kind of intrigue any more. The smell of danger was foreign to me now, and I found it unpleasant.

The small lump of the bird in my pocket tantalized me. I took it out again. It was a temptation to press the stud and let it settle things, or at least start them going, then and there.

After a while I noticed the proprietors of the shop staring at the silk of the wrappings. They backed off, apprehensive. I held out a coin and they shook their heads. "You are welcome to the drink," one of them said. "All we have is at your service. Only please go. Go quickly."

They would not touch the coins I offered. I thrust the bird in my pocket, swore and went. It was my second experience with being somehow tabu, and I didn't like it.

It was dusk when I realized I was being followed.

At first it was a glimpse out of the corner of my eye, a head seen too frequently for coincidence. It developed into a too-persistent footstep in uneven rhythm.

Tap-tap-tap. Tap-tap-tap.

I had my skean handy, but I had a hunch this wasn't anything I could settle with a skean. I ducked into a side street and waited.

Nothing.

I went on, laughing at my imagined fears.

Then, after a time, the soft, persistent footfall thudded behind me again.

I cut across a thieves market, dodging from stall to stall, cursed by old women selling hot fried goldfish, women in striped veils railing at me in their chiming talk when I brushed their rolled rugs with hasty feet. Far behind I heard the familiar uneven hurry: tap-tap-tap, tap-tap-tap.

I fled down a street where women sat on flower-decked balconies, their open lanterns flowing with fountains and rivulets of gold and orange fire. I raced through quiet streets where furred children crept to doors and watched me pass with great golden eyes that shone in the dark.

I dodged into an alley and lay there, breathing hard. Someone not two inches away said, "Are you one of us, brother?"

I muttered something surly, in his dialect, and a hand, reassuringly human, closed on my elbow. "This way."

Out of breath with long running, I let him lead me, meaning to break away after a few steps, apologize for mistaken identity and vanish, when a sound at the end of the street made me jerk stiff and listen.

Tap-tap-tap. Tap-tap-tap.

I let my arm relax in the hand that guided me, flung a fold of my shirtcloak over my face, and went along with my unknown guide.

Chapter Thirteen

I stumbled over steps, took a jolting stride downward, and found myself in a dim room jammed with dark figures, human and nonhuman.

The figures swayed in the darkness, chanting in a dialect not altogether familiar to me, a monotonous wailing chant, with a single recurrent phrase: "Kamaina! Kama-aina!" It began on a high note, descending in weird chromatics to the lowest tone the human ear could resolve.

The sound made me draw back. Even the Dry-towners shunned the orgiastic rituals of Kamaina. Earthmen have a reputation for getting rid of the more objectionable customs—by human standards—on any planet where they live. But they don't touch religions, and Kamaina, on the surface anyhow, was a religion.

I started to turn round and leave, as if I had inadvertently walked through the wrong door, but my conductor hauled on my arm, and I was wedged in too tight by now to risk a roughhouse. Trying to force my way out would only have called attention to me, and the first of the Secret Service maxims is; when in doubt, go along, keep quiet, and watch the other guy.

As my eyes adapted to the dim light, I saw that most of the crowd were Charin plainsmen or chaks. One or two wore Dry-town shirtcloaks, and I even thought I saw an Earthman in the crowd, though I was never sure and I fervently hope not. They were squatting around small crescent-shaped tables, and all intently gazing at a flickery spot of light at the front of the cellar. I saw an empty place at one table and dropped there, finding the floor soft, as if cushioned.

On each table, small smudging pastilles were burning, and from these cones of ash-tipped fire came the steamy, swimmy smoke that filled the darkness with strange colors. Beside me an immature chak girl was kneeling, her fettered hands strained tightly back at her sides, her naked breasts pierced for jeweled rings.

Beneath the pallid fur around her pointed ears, the exquisite animal face was quite mad. She whispered to me, but her dialect was so thick that I could follow only a few words, and would just as soon not have heard those few. An older chak grunted for silence and she subsided, swaying and crooning.

There were cups and decanters on all the tables, and a woman tilted pale, phosphorescent fluid into a cup and offered it to me. I took one sip, then another. It was cold and pleasantly tart, and not until the second swallow turned sweet on my tongue did I know what I tasted. I pretended to swallow while the woman's eyes were fixed on me, then somehow contrived to spill the filthy stuff down my shirt.

I was wary even of the fumes, but there was nothing else I could do. The stuff was shallavan, outlawed on every planet in the Terran Empire and every halfway decent planet outside it.

More and more figures, men and creatures, kept crowding into the cellar, which was not very large. The place looked like the worst nightmare of a drug-dreamer, ablaze with the colors of the smoking incense, the swaying crowd, and their monotonous cries. Quite suddenly there was a blaze of purple light and someone screamed in raving ecstasy: "Na ki na Nebran n'hai Kamaina!"

"Kamayeeeeeeeeeeeeeeeeeena!" shrilled the tranced mob.

An old man jumped up and started haranguing the crowd. I could just follow his dialect. He was talking about Terra. He was talking about riots. He was jabbering mystical gibberish which I couldn't understand and didn't want to understand, and rabble-rousing anti-Terran propaganda which I understood much too well.

Another blaze of lights and another long scream in chorus: "Kamayeeeeeeeeeeeeeeeeeeeena!"

Evarin stood in the blaze of the many-colored light.

The Toymaker, as I had seen him last, cat-smooth, gracefully alien, shrouded in a ripple of giddy crimsons. Behind him was a blackness. I waited till the painful blaze of lights abated, then, straining my eyes to see past him, I got my worst shock.

A woman stood there, naked to the waist, her hands ritually fettered with little chains that stirred and clashed musically as she moved stiff-legged in a frozen dream. Hair like black grass banded her brow and naked shoulders, and her eyes were crimson.

And the eyes lived in the dead dreaming face. They lived, and they were mad with terror although the lips curved in a gently tranced smile.

Miellyn.

Evarin was speaking in that dialect I barely understood. His arms were flung high and his cloak went spilling away from them, rippling like something alive. The jammed humans and nonhumans swayed and chanted and he swayed above them like an iridescent bug, weaving arms rippling back and forth, back and forth. I strained to catch his words.

"Our world ... an old world."

"Kamayeeeeena," whimpered the shrill chorus.

"... humans, humans, all humans would make slaves of us all, all save the Children of the Ape...."

I lost the thread for a moment. True. The Terran Empire has one small blind spot in otherwise sane policy, ignoring that nonhuman and human have lived placidly here for millennia: they placidly assumed that humans were everywhere the dominant race, as on Earth itself.

The Toymaker's weaving arms went on spinning, spinning. I rubbed my eyes to clear them of shallavan and incense. I hoped that what I saw was an illusion of the drug—something, something huge and dark, was hovering over the girl. She stood placidly, hands clasped on her chains, but her eyes writhed in the frozen calm of her face.

Then something—I can only call it a sixth sense—bore it on me that there was someone outside the door. I was perhaps the only creature there, except for Evarin, not drugged with shallavan, and perhaps that's all it was. But during the days in the Secret Service I'd had to develop some extra senses. Five just weren't enough for survival.

I knew somebody was fixing to break down that door, and I had a good idea why. I'd been followed, by the legate's orders, and, tracking me here, they'd gone away and brought back reinforcements.

Someone struck a blow on the door and a stentorian voice bawled, "Open up there, in the name of the Empire!"

The chanting broke in ragged quavers. Evarin stopped. Somewhere a woman screamed. The lights abruptly went out and a stampede started in the room. Women struck me with chains, men kicked, there were shrieks and howls. I thrust my way forward, butting with elbows and knees and shoulders.

A dusky emptiness yawned and I got a glimpse of sunlight and open sky and knew that Evarin had stepped through into somewhere and was gone. The banging on the door sounded like a whole regiment of Spaceforce out there. I dived toward the shimmer of little stars which marked Miellyn's tiara in the darkness, braving the black horror hovering over her, and touched rigid girl-flesh, cold as death.

I grabbed her and ducked sideways. This time it wasn't intuition—nine times out of ten, anyway, intuition is just a mental shortcut which adds up all the things which your subconscious has noticed while you were busy thinking about something else. Every native building on Wolf had concealed entrances and exits and I know where to look for them. This one was exactly where I expected. I pushed at it and found myself in a long, dim corridor.

The head of a woman peered from an opening door. She saw Miellyn's limp body hanging on my arm and her mouth widened in a silent scream. Then the head popped back out of sight and a door slammed. I heard the bolt slide. I ran for the end of the hall, the girl in my arms, thinking that this was where I came in, as far as Miellyn was concerned, and wondering why I bothered.

The door opened on a dark, peaceful street. One lonely moon was setting beyond the rooftops. I set Miellyn on her feet, but she moaned and crumpled against me. I put my shirtcloak around her bare shoulders. Judging by the noises and yells, we'd gotten out just in time. No one came out the exit behind us. Either the Spaceforce had plugged it or, more likely, everyone else in the cellar had been too muddled by drugs to know what was going on.

But it was only a few minutes, I knew, before Spaceforce would check the whole building for concealed escape holes. Suddenly, and irrelevantly, I found myself thinking of a day not too long ago, when I'd stood up in front of a unit-in-training of Spaceforce, introduced to them as an Intelligence expert on native towns, and solemnly warned them about concealed exits and entrances. I wondered, for half a minute, if it might not be simpler just to wait here and let them pick me up.

Then I hoisted Miellyn across my shoulders. She was heavier than she looked, and after a minute, half conscious, she began to struggle and moan. There was a chak-run cookshop down the street, a place I'd once known well, with an evil reputation and worse food, but it was quiet and stayed open all night. I turned in at the door, bending at the low lintel.

The place was smoke-filled and foul-smelling. I dumped Miellyn on a couch and sent the frowsy waiter for two bowls of noodles and coffee, handed him a few extra coins, and told him to leave us alone. He probably drew the worst possible inference—I saw his muzzle twitch at the smell of shallavan—but it was that kind of place anyhow. He drew down the shutters and went.

I stared at the unconscious girl, then shrugged and started on the noodles. My own head was still swimmy with the fumes, incense and drug, and I wanted it clear. I wasn't quite sure what I was going to do, but I had Evarin's right-hand girl, and I was going to use her.

The noodles were greasy and had a curious taste, but they were hot, and I ate all of one bowl before Miellyn stirred and whimpered and put up one hand, with a little clinking of chains, to her hair. The gesture was indefinably reminiscent of Dallisa, and for the first time I saw the likeness between them. It made me wary and yet curiously softened.

Finding she could not move freely, she rolled over, sat up and stared around in growing bewilderment and dismay.

"There was a sort of riot," I said. "I got you out. Evarin ditched you. And you can quit thinking what you're thinking, I put my shirtcloak on you because you were bare to the waist and it didn't look so good." I stopped to think that over, and amended: "I mean I couldn't haul you around the streets that way. It looked good enough."

To my surprise, she gave a shaky little giggle, and held out her fettered hands. "Will you?"

I broke her links and freed her. She rubbed her wrists as if they hurt her, then drew up her draperies, pinned them so that she was decently covered, and tossed back my shirtcloak. Her eyes were wide and soft in the light of the flickering stub of candle.

"O, Rakhal," she sighed. "When I saw you there—" She sat up, clasping her hands hard together, and when she continued her voice was curiously cold and controlled for anyone so childish. It was almost as cold as Dallisa's.

"If you've come from Kyral, I'm not going back. I'll never go back, and you may as well know it."

"I don't come from Kyral, and I don't care where you go. I don't care what you do." I suddenly realized that the last statement was wholly untrue, and to cover my confusion I shoved the remaining bowl of noodles at her.

"Eat."

She wrinkled her nose in fastidious disgust. "I'm not hungry."

"Eat it anyway. You're still half doped, and the food will clear your head." I picked up one mug of the coffee and drained it at a single swallow. "What were you doing in that disgusting den?"

Without warning she flung herself across the table at me, throwing her arms round my neck. Startled, I let her cling a moment, then reached up and firmly unfastened her hands.

"None of that now. I fell for it once, and it landed me in the middle of the mudpie."

But her fingers bit my shoulder.

"Rakhal, Rakhal, I tried to get away and find you. Have you still got the bird? You haven't set it off yet? Oh, don't, don't, don't, Rakhal, you don't know what Evarin is, you don't know what he's doing." The words spilled out of her like floodwaters. "He's won so many of you, don't let him have you too, Rakhal. They call you an honest man, you worked once for Terra, the

Terrans would believe you if you went to them and told them what he—Rakhal, take me to the Terran Zone, take me there, take me there where they'll protect me from Evarin."

At first I tried to stop her, question her, then waited and let the torrent of entreaty run on and on. At last, exhausted and breathless, she lay quietly against my shoulder, her head fallen forward. The musty reek of shallavan mingled with the flower scent of her hair.

"Kid," I said heavily at last, "you and your Toymaker have both got me wrong. I'm not Rakhal Sensar."

"You're not?" She drew back, regarding me in dismay. Her eyes searched every inch of me, from the gray streak across my forehead to the scar running down into my collar. "Then who—"

"Race Cargill. Terran Intelligence."

She stared, her mouth wide like a child's.

Then she laughed. She laughed! At first I thought she was hysterical. I stared at her in consternation. Then, as her wide eyes met mine, with all the mischief of the nonhuman which has mingled into the human here, all the circular complexities of Wolf illogic behind the woman in them, I started to laugh too.

I threw back my head and roared, until we were clinging together and gasping with mirth like a pair of raving fools. The chak waiter came to the door and stared at us, and I roared "Get the hell out," between spasms of crazy laughter.

Then she was wiping her face, tears of mirth still dripping down her cheeks, and I was frowning bleakly into the empty bowls.

"Cargill," she said hesitantly, "you can take me to the Terrans where Rakhal—"

"Hell's bells," I exploded. "I can't take you anywhere, girl. I've got to find Rakhal—" I stopped in midsentence and looked at her clearly for the first time.

"Child, I'll see that you're protected, if I can. But I'm afraid you've walked from the trap to the cookpot. There isn't a house in Charin that will hold me. I've been thrown out twice today."

She nodded. "I don't know how the word spreads, but it happens, in nonhuman parts. I think they can see trouble written in a human face, or smell it on the wind." She fell silent, her face propped sleepily between her hands, her hair falling in tangles. I took one of her hands in mine and turned it over.

It was a fine hand, with birdlike bones and soft rose-tinted nails; but the lines and hardened places around the knuckles reminded me that she, too, came from the cold austerity of the salt Dry-towns. After a moment she flushed and drew her hand from mine.

"What are you thinking, Cargill?" she asked, and for the first time I heard her voice sobered, without the coquetry, which must after all have been a very thin veneer.

I answered her simply and literally. "I am thinking of Dallisa. I thought you were very different, and yet, I see that you are very like her."

I thought she would question what I knew of her sister, but she let it pass in silence. After a time she said, "Yes, we were twins." Then, after a long silence, she added, "But she was always much the older."

And that was all I ever knew of whatever obscure pressures had shaped Dallisa into an austere and tragic Clytemnestra, and Miellyn into a pixie runaway.

Outside the drawn shutters, dawn was brightening. Miellyn shivered, drawing her thin draperies around her bare throat. I glanced at the little rim of jewels that starred her hair and said, "You'd better take those off and hide them. They alone would be enough to have you hauled into an alley and strangled, in this part of Charin." I hauled the bird Toy from my pocket and slapped it on the greasy table, still wrapped in its silk. "I don't suppose you know which of us this thing is set to kill?"

"I know nothing about the Toys."

"You seem to know plenty about the Toymaker."

"I thought so. Until last night." I looked at the rigid, clamped mouth and thought that if she were really as soft and delicate as she looked, she would have wept. Then she struck her small hand on the tabletop and burst out, "It's not a religion. It isn't even an honest movement for freedom! Its a—a front for smuggling, and drugs, and—and every other filthy thing!

"Believe it or not, when I left Shainsa, I thought Nebran was the answer to the way the Terrans were strangling us! Now I know there are worse things on Wolf than the Terran Empire! I've heard of Rakhal Sensar, and whatever you may think of Rakhal, he's too decent to be mixed up in anything like this!"

"Suppose you tell me what's really going on," I suggested. She couldn't add much to what I knew already, but the last fragments of the pattern were beginning to settle into place. Rakhal, seeking the matter transmitter and some key to the nonhuman sciences of Wolf—I knew now what the city of

Silent Ones had reminded me of!—had somehow crossed the path of the Toymaker.

Evarin's words now made sense: "You were clever at evading our surveillance—for a while." Possibly, though I'd never know, Cuinn had been keeping one foot in each camp, working for Kyral and for Evarin. The Toymaker, knowing of Rakhal's anti-Terran activities, had believed he would make a valuable ally and had taken steps to secure his help.

Juli herself had given me the clue: "He smashed Rindy's Toys." Out of the context it sounded like the work of a madman. Now, having encountered Evarin's workshop, it made plain good sense.

And I think I had known all along that Rakhal could not have been playing Evarin's game. He might have turned against Terra—though now I was beginning even to doubt that—and certainly he'd have killed me if he found me. But he would have done it himself, and without malice. Killed without malice—that doesn't make sense in any of the languages of Terra. But it made sense to me.

Miellyn had finished her brief recitation and was drowsing, her head pillowed on the table. The reddish light was growing, and I realized that I was waiting for dawn as, days ago, I had waited for sunset in Shainsa, with every nerve stretched to the breaking point. It was dawn of the third morning, and this bird lying on the table before me must fly or, far away in the Kharsa, another would fly at Juli.

I said, "There's some distance limitation on this one, I understand, since I have to be fairly near its object. If I lock it in a steel box and drop it in the desert, I'll guarantee it won't bother anybody. I don't suppose you'd have a shot at stealing the other one for me?"

She raised her head, eyes flashing. "Why should you worry about Rakhal's wife?" she flared, and for no good reason it occurred to me that she was jealous. "I might have known Evarin wouldn't shoot in the dark! Rakhal's wife, that Earthwoman, what do you care for her?"

It seemed important to set her straight. I explained that Juli was my sister, and saw a little of the tension fade from her face, but not all. Remembering the custom of the Dry-towns, I was not wholly surprised when she added, jealously, "When I heard of your feud, I guessed it was over that woman!"

"But not in the way you think," I said. Juli had been part of it, certainly. Even then I had not wanted her to turn her back on her world, but if Rakhal had remained with Terra, I would have accepted his marriage to Juli. Accepted it. I'd have rejoiced. God knows we had been closer than brothers, those years in the Dry-towns. And then, before Miellyn's flashing eyes, I suddenly faced my secret hate, my secret fear. No, the quarrel had not been all Rakhal's doing.

He had not turned his back, unexplained on Terra. In some unrecognized fashion, I had done my best to drive him away. And when he had gone, I had banished a part of myself as well, and thought I could end the struggle by saying it didn't exist. And now, facing what I had done to all of us, I knew that my revenge—so long sought, so dearly cherished—must be abandoned.

"We still have to deal with the bird," I said. "It's a gamble, with all the cards wild." I could dismantle it, and trust to luck that Wolf illogic didn't include a tamper mechanism. But that didn't seem worth the risk.

"First I've got to find Rakhal. If I set the bird free and it killed him, it wouldn't settle anything." For I could not kill Rakhal. Not, now, because I knew life would be a worse punishment than death. But because—I knew it, now—if Rakhal died, Juli would die, too. And if I killed him I'd be killing the best part of myself. Somehow Rakhal and I must strike a balance between our two worlds, and try to build a new one from them.

"And I can't sit here and talk any longer. I haven't time to take you—" I stopped, remembering the spaceport cafe at the edge of the Kharsa. There was a street-shrine, or matter transmitter, right there, across the street from the Terran HQ. All these years....

"You know your way in the transmitters. You can go there in a second or two." She could warn Juli, tell Magnusson. But when I suggested this, giving her a password that would take her straight to the top, she turned white. "All jumps have to be made through the Mastershrine."

I stopped and thought about that.

"Where is Evarin likely to be, right now?"

She gave a nervous shudder. "He's everywhere!"

"Rubbish! He's not omniscient! Why, you little fool, he didn't even recognize me. He thought I was Rakhal!" I wasn't too sure, myself, but Miellyn needed reassurance. "Or take me to the Mastershrine. I can find Rakhal in that scanning device of Evarin's." I saw refusal in her face and pushed on, "If Evarin's there, I'll prove he's fallible enough with a skean in his throat! And here"—I thrust the Toy into her hand—"hang on to this, will you?"

She put it matter-of-factly into her draperies. "I don't mind that. But to the shrine—" Her voice quivered, and I stood up and pushed at the table.

"Let's get going. Where's the nearest street-shrine?"

"No, no! Oh, I don't dare!"

"You've got to." I saw the chak who owned the place edging round the door again and said, "There's no use arguing, Miellyn." When she had readjusted her robes a little while ago, she had pinned them so that the flat sprawl of the Nebran embroideries was over her breasts. I put a finger against them, not in a sensuous gesture, and said, "The minute they see these, they'll throw us out of here, too."

"If you knew what I know of Nebran, you wouldn't want me to go near the Mastershrine again!" There was that faint coquettishness in her sidewise smile.

And suddenly I realized that I didn't want her to. But she was not Dallisa and she could not sit in cold dignity while her world fell into ruin. Miellyn must fight for the one she wanted.

And then some of that primitive male hostility which lives in every man came to the surface, and I gripped her arm until she whimpered. Then I said, in the Shainsan which still comes to my tongue when moved or angry, "Damn it, you're going. Have you forgotten that if it weren't for me you'd have been torn to pieces by that raving mob, or something worse?"

That did it. She pulled away and I saw again, beneath the veneer of petulant coquetry, that fierce and untamable insolence of the Dry-towner. The more fierce and arrogant, in this girl, because she had burst her fettered hands free and shaken off the ruin of the past.

I was seized with a wildly inappropriate desire to seize her, crush her in my arms, taste the red honey of that teasing mouth. The effort of mastering the impulse made me rough.

I shoved at her and said, "Come on. Let's get there before Evarin does."

Chapter Fourteen

Outside in the streets it was full day, and the color and life of Charin had subsided into listlessness again, a dim morning dullness and silence. Only a few men lounged wearily in the streets, as if the sun had sapped their energy. And always the pale fleecy-haired children, human and furred nonhuman, played their mysterious games on the curbs and gutters and staring at us with neither curiosity nor malice.

Miellyn was shaking when she set her feet into the patterned stones of the street-shrine.

"Scared, Miellyn?"

"I know Evarin. You don't. But"—her mouth twitched in a pitiful attempt at the old mischief—"when I am with a great and valorous Earthman...."

"Cut it out," I growled, and she giggled. "You'll have to stand closer to me. The transmitters are meant only for one person."

I stooped and put my arms round her. "Like this?"

"Like this," she whispered, pressing herself against me. A staggering whirl of dizzy darkness swung round my head. The street vanished. After an instant the floor steadied and we stepped into the terminal room in the Mastershrine, under a skylight dim with the last red slant of sunset. Distant hammering noises rang in my ears.

Miellyn whispered, "Evarin's not here, but he might jump through at any second." I wasn't listening.

"Where is this place, Miellyn? Where on the planet?"

"No one knows but Evarin, I think. There are no doors. Anyone who goes in or out, jumps through the transmitter." She pointed. "The scanning device is in there, we'll have to go through the workroom."

She was patting her crushed robes into place, smoothing her hair with fastidious fingers. "I don't suppose you have a comb? I've no time to go to my own—"

I'd known she was a vain and pampered brat, but this passed all reason, and I said so, exploding at her. She looked at me as if I wasn't quite intelligent. "The Little Ones, my friend, notice things. You are quite enough of a roughneck, but if I, Nebran's priestess, walk through their workroom all blown about and looking like the tag end of an orgy in Ardcarran...."

Abashed, I fished in a pocket and offered her a somewhat battered pocket comb. She looked at it distastefully but used it to good purpose, smoothing her hair swiftly, rearranging her loose-pinned robe so that the worst of the tears and stains were covered, and giving me, meanwhile, an artless and rather tempting view of some delicious curvature. She replaced the starred tiara on her ringlets and finally opened the door of the workroom and we walked through.

Not for years had I known that particular sensation—thousands of eyes, boring holes in the center of my back somewhere. There were eyes; the round inhuman orbs of the dwarf chaks, the faceted stare of the prism eyes of the Toys. The workroom wasn't a hundred feet long, but it felt longer than a good many miles I've walked. Here and there the dwarfs murmured an obsequious greeting to Miellyn, and she made some lighthearted answer.

She had warned me to walk as if I had every right to be there, and I strode after her as if we were simply going to an agreed-on meeting in the next room. But I was drenched with cold sweat before the farther door finally closed, safe and blessedly opaque, behind us. Miellyn, too, was shaking with fright, and I put a hand on her arm.

"Steady, kid. Where's the scanner?"

She touched the panel I'd seen. "I'm not sure I can focus it accurately. Evarin never let me touch it."

This was a fine time to tell me that. "How does it work?"

"It's an adaptation of the transmitter principle. It lets you see anywhere, but without jumping. It uses a tracer mechanism like the one in the Toys. If Rakhal's electrical-impulse pattern were on file—just a minute." She fished out the bird Toy and unwrapped it. "Here's how we find out which of you this is keyed to."

I looked at the fledgling bird, lying innocently in her palm, as she pushed aside the feathers, exposing a tiny crystal. "If it's keyed to you, you'll see yourself in this, as if the screen were a mirror. If it's keyed to Rakhal...."

She touched the crystal to the surface of the screen. Little flickers of snow wavered and danced. Then, abruptly, we were looking down from a height at the lean back of a man in a leather jacket. Slowly he turned. I saw the familiar set of his shoulders, saw the back of his head come into an aquiline profile, and the profile turn slowly into a scarred, seared mask more hideously claw-marked and disfigured than my own.

"Rakhal," I muttered. "Shift the focus if you can, Miellyn, get a look out the window or something. Charin's a big city. If we could get a look at a landmark—"

Rakhal was talking soundlessly, his lips moving as he spoke to someone out of sight range of the scanning device. Abruptly Miellyn said, "There." She had caught a window in the sight field of the pane. I could see a high pylon and two of three uprights that looked like a bridge, just outside. I said, "It's the Bridge of Summer Snows. I know where he is now. Turn it off, Miellyn, we can find him—" I was turning away when Miellyn screamed.

"Look!"

Rakhal had turned his back on the scanner and for the first time I could see who he was talking to. A hunched, catlike shoulder twisted; a sinuous neck, a high-held head that was not quite human.

"Evarin!" I swore. "That does it. He knows now that I'm not Rakhal, if he didn't know it all along! Come on, girl, we're getting out of here!"

This time there was no pretense of normality as we dashed through the workroom. Fingers dropped from half-completed Toys as they stared after us. Toys! I wanted to stop and smash them all. But if we hurried, we might find Rakhal. And, with luck, we would find Evarin with him.

And then I was going to bang their heads together. I'd reached a saturation point on adventure. I'd had all I wanted. I realized that I'd been up all night, that I was exhausted. I wanted to murder and smash, and wanted to fall down somewhere and go to sleep, all at once. We banged the workroom door shut and I took time to shove a heavy divan against it, blockading it.

Miellyn stared. "The Little Ones would not harm me," she began. "I am sacrosanct."

I wasn't sure. I had a notion her status had changed plenty, beginning when I saw her chained and drugged, and standing under the hovering horror. But I didn't say so.

"Maybe. But there's nothing sacred about me!"

She was already inside the recess where the Toad God squatted. "There is a street-shrine just beyond the Bridge of Summer Snows. We can jump directly there." Abruptly she froze in my arms, with a convulsive shudder.

"Evarin! Hold me, tight—he's jumping in! Quick!"

Space reeled round us, and then....

Can you split instantaneousness into fragments? It didn't make sense, but so help me, that's what happened. And everything that happened, occurred within less than a second. We landed in the street-shrine. I could see the pylon and the bridge and the rising sun of Charin. Then there was the giddy internal wrenching, a blast of icy air whistled round us, and we were gazing out at the Polar mountains, ringed in their eternal snow.

Miellyn clutched at me. "Pray! Pray to the Gods of Terra, if there are any!"

She clung so violently that it felt as if her small body was trying to push through me and come out the other side. I hung on tight. Miellyn knew what she was doing in the transmitter; I was just along for the ride and I didn't relish the thought of being dropped off somewhere in that black limbo we traversed.

We jumped again, the sickness of disorientation forcing a moan from the girl, and darkness shivered round us. I looked on an unfamiliar street of black night and dust-bleared stars. She whimpered, "Evarin knows what I'm doing. He's jumping us all over the planet. He can work the controls with his mind. Psychokinetics—I can do it a little, but I never dared—oh, hang on tight!"

Then began one of the most amazing duels ever fought. Miellyn would make some tiny movement, and we would be falling, blind and dizzy, through blackness. Halfway through the giddiness, a new direction would wrench us and we would be thrust elsewhere, and look out into a new street.

One instant I smelled hot coffee from the spaceport cafe near the Kharsa. An instant later it was blinding noon, with crimson fronds waving above us and a dazzle of water. We flicked in and out of the salty air of Shainsa, glimpsed flowers on a Daillon street, moonlight, noon, red twilight flickered and went, shot through with the terrible giddiness of hyperspace.

Then suddenly I caught a second glimpse of the bridge and the pylon; a moment's oversight had landed us for an instant in Charin. The blackness started to reel down, but my reflexes are fast and I made one swift, scrabbling step forward. We lurched, sprawled, locked together, on the stones of the Bridge of Summer Snows. Battered, and bruised, and bloody, we were still alive, and where we wanted to be.

I lifted Miellyn to her feet. Her eyes were dazed with pain. The ground swayed and rocked under our feet as we fled along the bridge. At the far end, I looked up at the pylon. Judging from its angle, we couldn't be more than a hundred feet from the window through which I'd seen that landmark in the scanner. In this street there was a wineshop, a silk market, and a small private house. I walked up and banged on the door.

Silence. I knocked again and had time to wonder if we'd find ourselves explaining things to some uninvolved stranger. Then I heard a child's high voice, and a deep familiar voice hushing it. The door opened, just a crack, to reveal part of a scarred face.

It drew into a hideous grin, then relaxed.

"I thought it might be you, Cargill. You've taken at least three days longer than I figured, getting here. Come on in," said Rakhal Sensar.

Chapter Fifteen

He hadn't changed much in six years. His face was worse than mine; he hadn't had the plastic surgeons of Terran Intelligence doing their best for him. His mouth, I thought fleetingly, must hurt like hell when he drew it up into the kind of grin he was grinning now. His eyebrows, thick and fierce with gray in them, went up as he saw Miellyn; but he backed away to let us enter, and shut the door behind us.

The room was bare and didn't look as if it had been lived in much. The floor was stone, rough-laid, a single fur rug laid before a brazier. A little girl was sitting on the rug, drinking from a big double-handled mug, but she scrambled to her feet as we came in, and backed against the wall, looking at us with wide eyes.

She had pale-red hair like Juli's, cut straight in a fringe across her forehead, and she was dressed in a smock of dyed red fur that almost matched her hair. A little smear of milk like a white moustache clung to her upper lip where she had forgotten to wipe her mouth. She was about five years old, with deep-set dark eyes like Juli's, that watched me gravely without surprise or fear; she evidently knew who I was.

"Rindy," Rakhal said quietly, not taking his eyes from me. "Go into the other room."

Rindy didn't move, still staring at me. Then she moved toward Miellyn, looking up intently not at the woman, but at the pattern of embroideries across her dress. It was very quiet, until Rakhal added, in a gentle and curiously moderate voice, "Do you still carry a skean, Race?"

I shook my head. "There's an ancient proverb on Terra, about blood being thicker than water, Rakhal. That's Juli's daughter. I'm not going to kill her father right before her eyes." My rage spilled over then, and I bellowed, "To hell with your damned Dry-town feuds and your filthy Toad God and all the rest of it!"

Rakhal said harshly, "Rindy. I told you to get out."

"She needn't go." I took a step toward the little girl, a wary eye on Rakhal. "I don't know quite what you're up to, but it's nothing for a child to be mixed up in. Do what you damn please. I can settle with you any time.

"The first thing is to get Rindy out of here. She belongs with Juli and, damn it, that's where she's going." I held out my arms to the little girl and said, "It's over, Rindy, whatever he's done to you. Your mother sent me to find you. Don't you want to go to your mother?"

Rakhal made a menacing gesture and warned, "I wouldn't—"

Miellyn darted swiftly between us and caught up the child in her arms. Rindy began to struggle noiselessly, kicking and whimpering, but Miellyn took two quick steps, and flung an inner door open. Rakhal took a stride toward her. She whirled on him, fighting to control the furious little girl, and gasped, "Settle it between you, without the baby watching!"

Through the open door I briefly saw a bed, a child's small dresses hanging on a hook, before Miellyn kicked the door shut and I heard a latch being fastened. Behind the closed door Rindy broke into angry screams, but I put my back against the door.

"She's right. We'll settle it between the two of us. What have you done to that child?"

"If you thought—" Rakhal stopped himself in midsentence and stood watching me without moving for a minute. Then he laughed.

"You're as stupid as ever, Race. Why, you fool, I knew Juli would run straight to you, if she was scared enough. I knew it would bring you out of hiding. Why, you damned fool!" He stood mocking me, but there was a strained fury, almost a frenzy of contempt behind the laughter.

"You filthy coward, Race! Six years hiding in the Terran zone. Six years, and I gave you six months! If you'd had the guts to walk out after me, after I rigged that final deal to give you the chance, we could have gone after the biggest thing on Wolf. And we could have brought it off together, instead of spending years spying and dodging and hunting! And now, when I finally get you out of hiding, all you want to do is run back where you'll be safe! I thought you had more guts!"

"Not for Evarin's dirty work!"

Rakhal swore hideously. "Evarin! Do you really believe—I might have known he'd get to you too! That girl—and you've managed to wreck all I did there, too!" Suddenly, so swiftly my eyes could hardly follow, he whipped out his skean and came at me. "Get away from that door!"

I stood my ground. "You'll have to kill me first. And I won't fight you, Rakhal. We'll settle this, but we'll do it my way for once, like Earthmen."

"Son of the Ape! Get your skean out, you stinking coward!"

"I won't do it, Rakhal." I stood and defied him. I had outmaneuvered Dry-towners in a shegri bet. I knew Rakhal, and I knew he would not knife an unarmed man. "We fought once with the kifirgh and it didn't settle anything. This time we'll do it my way. I threw my skean away before I came here. I won't fight."

He thrust at me. Even I could see that the blow was a feint, and I had a flashing, instantaneous memory of Dallisa's threat to drive the knife through my palms. But even while I commanded myself to stand steady, sheer reflex threw me forward, grabbing at his wrist and the knife.

Between my grappling hand he twisted and I felt the skean drive home, rip through my jacket with a tearing sound; felt the thin fine line of touch, not pain yet, as it sliced flesh. Then pain burned through my ribs and I felt hot blood, and I wanted to kill Rakhal, wanted to get my hands around his throat and kill him with them. And at the same time I was raging because I didn't want to fight the crazy fool, I wasn't even mad at him.

Miellyn flung the door open, shrieking, and suddenly the Toy, released, was darting a small whirring droning horror, straight at Rakhal's eyes. I yelled. But there was no time even to warn him. I bent and butted him in the stomach. He grunted, doubled up in agony and fell out of the path of the diving Toy. It whirred in frustration, hovered.

He writhed in agony, drawing up his knees, clawing at his shirt, while I turned on Miellyn in immense fury—and stopped. Hers had been a move of desperation, an instinctive act to restore the balance between a weaponless man and one who had a knife. Rakhal gasped, in a hoarse voice with all the breath gone from it:

"Didn't want to use. Rather fight clean—" Then he opened his closed fist and suddenly there were two of the little whirring droning horrors in the room and this one was diving at me, and as I threw myself headlong to the floor the last puzzle-piece fell into place: Evarin had made the same bargain with Rakhal as with me!

I rolled over, dodging. Behind me in the room there was a child's shrill scream: "Daddy! Daddy!" And abruptly the birds collapsed in midair and went limp. They fell to the floor like dropping stones and lay there quivering. Rindy dashed across the room, her small skirts flying, and grabbed up one of the terrible vicious things in either hand.

"Rindy!" I bellowed. "No!"

She stood shaking, tears pouring down her round cheeks, a Toy squeezed tight in either hand. Dark veins stood out almost black on her fair temples.

"Break them, Daddy," she implored in a little thread of a voice. "Break them, quick. I can't hang on...."

Rakhal staggered to his feet like a drunken man and snatched one of the Toys, grinding it under his heel. He made a grab at the second, reeled and drew an anguished breath. He crumpled up, clutching at his belly where I'd butted him. The bird screamed like a living thing.

Breaking my paralysis of horror I leaped up, ran across the room, heedless of the searing pain along my side. I snatched the bird from Rindy and it screamed and shrilled and died as my foot crunched the tiny feathers. I stamped the still-moving thing into an amorphous mess and kept on stamping and smashing until it was only a heap of powder.

Rakhal finally managed to haul himself upright again. His face was so pale that the scars stood out like fresh burns.

"That was a foul blow, Race, but I—I know why you did it." He stopped and breathed for a minute. Then he muttered, "You ... saved my life, you know. Did you know you were doing it, when you did it?"

Still breathing hard, I nodded. Done knowingly, it meant an end of blood-feud. However we had wronged each other, whatever the pledges. I spoke the words that confirmed it and ended it, finally and forever:

"There is a life between us. Let it stand for a death."

Miellyn was standing in the doorway, her hands pressed to her mouth, her eyes wide. She said shakily, "You're walking around with a knife in your ribs, you fool!"

Rakhal whirled and with a quick jerk he pulled the skean loose. It had simply been caught in my shirtcloak, in a fold of the rough cloth. He pulled it away, glanced at the red tip, then relaxed. "Not more than an inch deep," he said. Then, angrily, defending himself: "You did it yourself, you ape. I was trying to get rid of the knife when you jumped me."

But I knew that and he knew I knew it. He turned and scooped up Rindy, who was sobbing noisily. She dug her head into his shoulder and I made out her strangled words. "The other Toys hurt you when I was mad at you...." she sobbed, rubbing her fists against smeared cheeks. "I—I wasn't that mad at you. I wasn't that mad at anybody, not even ... him."

Rakhal pressed his hand against his daughter's fleecy hair and said, looking at me over her head, "The Toys activate a child's subconscious resentments against his parents—I found out that much. That also means a child can control them for a few seconds. No adult can." A stranger would have seen no change in his expression, but I knew him, and saw.

"Juli said you threatened Rindy."

He chuckled and set the child on her feet. "What else could I say that would have scared Juli enough to send her running to you? Juli's proud, almost as proud as you are, you stiff-necked Son of the Ape." The insult did not sting me now.

"Come on, sit down and let's decide what to do, now we've finished up the old business." He looked remotely at Miellyn and said, "You must be Dallisa's sister? I don't suppose your talents include knowing how to make coffee?"

They didn't, but with Rindy's help Miellyn managed, and while they were out of the room Rakhal explained briefly. "Rindy has rudimentary ESP. I've never had it myself, but I could teach her something—not much—about how to use it. I've been on Evarin's track ever since that business of The Lisse.

"I'd have got it sooner, if you were still working with me, but I couldn't do anything as a Terran agent, and I had to be kicked out so thoroughly that the others wouldn't be afraid I was still working secretly for Terra. For a long time I was just chasing rumors, but when Rindy got big enough to look in the crystals of Nebran, I started making some progress.

"I was afraid to tell Juli; her best safety was the fact that she didn't know anything. She's always been a stranger in the Dry-towns." He paused, then said with honest self-evaluation, "Since I left the Secret Service I've been a stranger there myself."

I asked, "What about Dallisa?"

"Twins have some ESP to each other. I knew Miellyn had gone to the Toymaker. I tried to get Dallisa to find out where Miellyn had gone, learn more about it. Dallisa wouldn't risk it, but Kyral saw me with Dallisa and thought it was Miellyn. That put him on my tail, too, and I had to leave Shainsa. I was afraid of Kyral," he added soberly. "Afraid of what he'd do. I couldn't do anything without Rindy and I knew if I told Juli what I was doing, she'd take Rindy away into the Terran Zone, and I'd be as good as dead."

As he talked, I began to realize how vast a web Evarin and the underground organization of Nebran had spread for us. "Evarin was here today. What for?"

Rakhal laughed mirthlessly. "He's been trying to get us to kill each other off. That would get rid of us both. He wants to turn over Wolf to the nonhumans entirely, I think he's sincere enough, but"—he spread his hands helplessly—"I can't sit by and see it."

I asked point-blank, "Are you working for Terra? Or for the Dry-towns? Or any of the anti-Terran movements?"

"I'm working for me", he said with a shrug. "I don't think much of the Terran Empire, but one planet can't fight a galaxy. Race, I want just one thing. I want the Dry-towns and the rest of Wolf, to have a voice in their own government. Any planet which makes a substantial contribution to galactic science, by the laws of the Terran Empire, is automatically given the status of an independent commonwealth.

"If a man from the Dry-towns discovers something like a matter transmitter, Wolf gets dominion status. But Evarin and his gang want to keep it secret, keep it away from Terra, keep it locked up in places like Canarsa! Somebody has to get it away from them. And if I do it, I get a nice fat bonus, and an official position."

I believed that, where I would have suspected too much protestation of altruism. Rakhal tossed it aside.

"You've got Miellyn to take you through the transmitters. Go back to the Mastershrine, and tell Evarin that Race Cargill is dead. In the Trade City they think I'm Cargill, and I can get in and out as I choose—sorry if it caused you trouble, but it was the safest thing I could think of—and I'll 'vise Magnusson and have him send soldiers to guard the street-shrines. Evarin might try to escape through one of them."

I shook my head. "Terra hasn't enough men on all Wolf to cover the street-shrines in Charin alone. And I can't go back with Miellyn." I explained. Rakhal pursed his lips and whistled when I described the fight in the transmitter.

"You have all the luck, Cargill! I've never been near enough even to be sure how they work—and I'll bet you didn't begin to understand! We'll have to do it the hard way, then. It won't be the first time we've bulled our way through a tight place! We'll face Evarin in his own hideout! If Rindy's with us, we needn't worry."

I was willing to let him assume command, but I protested, "You'd take a child into that—that—"

"What else can we do? Rindy can control the Toys, and neither you nor I can do that, if Evarin should decide to throw his whole arsenal at us." He called Rindy and spoke softly to her. She looked from her father to me, and back again to her father, then smiled and stretched out her hand to me.

Before we ventured into the street, Rakhal scowled at the sprawled embroideries of Miellyn's robe. He said, "In those things you show up like a snowfall in Shainsa. If you go out in them, you could be mobbed. Hadn't you better get rid of them now?"

"I can't," she protested. "They're the keys to the transmitter!"

Rakhal looked at the conventionalized idols with curiosity, but said only, "Cover them up in the street, then. Rindy, find her something to put over her dress."

When we reached the street-shrine, Miellyn admonished: "Stand close together on the stones. I'm not sure we can all make the jump at once, but we'll have to try."

Rakhal picked up Rindy and hoisted her to his shoulder. Miellyn dropped the cloak she had draped over the pattern of the Nebran embroideries, and we crowded close together. The street swayed and vanished and I felt the now-familiar dip and swirl of blackness before the world straightened out again. Rindy was whimpering, dabbing smeary fists at her face. "Daddy, my nose is bleeding...."

Miellyn hastily bent and wiped the blood from the snubby nose. Rakhal gestured impatiently.

"The workroom. Wreck everything you see. Rindy, if anything starts to come at us, you stop it. Stop it quick. And"—he bent and took the little face between his hands—"chiya, remember they're not toys, no matter how pretty they are."

Her grave gray eyes blinked, and she nodded.

Rakhal flung open the door of the elves' workshop with a shout. The ringing of the anvils shattered into a thousand dissonances as I kicked over a workbench and half-finished Toys crashed in confusion to the floor.

The dwarfs scattered like rabbits before our assault of destruction. I smashed tools, filigree, jewels, stamping everything with my heavy boots. I shattered glass, caught up a hammer and smashed crystals. There was a wild exhilaration to it.

A tiny doll, proportioned like a woman, dashed toward me, shrilling in a supersonic shriek. I put my foot on her and ground the life out of her, and she screamed like a living woman as she came apart. Her blue eyes rolled from her head and lay on the floor watching me. I crushed the blue jewels under my heel.

Rakhal swung a tiny hound by the tail. Its head shattered into debris of almost-invisible gears and wheels. I caught up a chair and wrecked a glass cabinet of parts with it, swinging furiously. A berserk madness of smashing and breaking had laid hold on me.

I was drunk with crushing and shattering and ruining, when I heard Miellyn scream a warning and turned to see Evarin standing in the doorway. His green cat-eyes blazed with rage. Then he raised both hands in a sudden, sardonic gesture, and with a loping, inhuman glide, raced for the transmitter.

"Rindy," Rakhal panted, "can you block the transmitter?"

Instead Rindy shrieked. "We've got to get out! The roof is falling down! The house is going to fall down on us! The roof, look at the roof!"

I looked up, transfixed by horror. I saw a wide rift open, saw the skylight shatter and break, and daylight pouring through the cracking walls, Rakhal snatched Rindy up, protecting her from the falling debris with his head and shoulders. I grabbed Miellyn round the waist and we ran for the rift in the buckling wall.

We shoved through just before the roof caved in and the walls collapsed, and we found ourselves standing on a bare grassy hillside, looking down in shock and horror as below us, section after section of what had been apparently bare hill and rock caved in and collapsed into dusty rubble.

Miellyn screamed hoarsely. "Run. Run, hurry!"

I didn't understand, but I ran. I ran, my sides aching, blood streaming from the forgotten flesh-wound in my side. Miellyn raced beside me and Rakhal stumbled along, carrying Rindy.

Then the shock of a great explosion rocked the ground, hurling me down full length, Miellyn falling on top of me. Rakhal went down on his knees. Rindy was crying loudly. When I could see straight again, I looked down at the hillside.

There was nothing left of Evarin's hideaway or the Mastershrine of Nebran except a great, gaping hole, still oozing smoke and thick black dust. Miellyn said aloud, dazed, "So that's what he was going to do!"

It fitted the peculiar nonhuman logic of the Toymaker. He'd covered the traces.

"Destroyed!" Rakhal raged. "All destroyed! The workrooms, the science of the Toys, the matter transmitter—the minute we find it, it's destroyed!" He beat his fists furiously. "Our one chance to learn—"

"We were lucky to get out alive," said Miellyn quietly. "Where on the planet are we, I wonder?"

I looked down the hillside, and stared in amazement. Spread out on the hillside below us lay the Kharsa, topped by the white skyscraper of the HQ.

"I'll be damned," I said, "right here. We're home. Rakhal, you can go down and make your peace with the Terrans, and Juli. And you, Miellyn—" Before the others, I could not say what I was thinking, but I put my hand on her shoulder and kept it there. She smiled, shakily, with a hint of her old mischief. "I can't go into the Terran Zone looking like this, can I? Give me that comb again. Rakhal, give me your shirtcloak, my robes are torn."

"You vain, stupid female, worrying about a thing like that at a time like this!" Rakhal's look was like murder. I put my comb in her hand, then suddenly saw something in the symbols across her breasts. Before this I had seen only the conventionalized and intricate glyph of the Toad God. But now—

I reached out and ripped the cloth away.

"Cargill!" she protested angrily, crimsoning, covering her bare breasts with both hands. "Is this the place? And before a child, too!"

I hardly heard. "Look!" I exclaimed. "Rakhal, look at the symbols embroidered into the glyph of the God! You can read the old nonhuman glyphs. You did it in the city of The Lisse. Miellyn said they were the key to the transmitters! I'll bet the formula is written out there for anyone to read!

"Anyone, that is, who can read it! I can't, but I'll bet the formula equations for the transmitters are carved on every Toad God glyph on Wolf. Rakhal, it makes sense. There are two ways of hiding something. Either keep it locked away, or hide it right out in plain sight. Whoever bothers even to look at a conventionalized Toad God? There are so many billions of them...."

He bent his head over the embroideries, and when he looked up his face was flushed. "I believe—by the chains of Sharra, I believe you have it, Race! It may take years to work out the glyphs, but I'll do it, or die trying!" His scarred and hideous face looked almost handsome in exultation, and I grinned at him.

"If Juli leaves enough of you, once she finds out how you maneuvered her. Look, Rindy's fallen asleep on the grass there. Poor kid, we'd better get her down to her mother."

"Right." Rakhal thrust the precious embroidery into his shirtcloak, then cradled his sleeping daughter in his arms. I watched him with a curious emotion I could not identify. It seemed to pinpoint some great change, either in Rakhal or myself. It's not difficult to visualize one's sister with children, but there was something, some strange incongruity in the sight of Rakhal carrying the little girl, carefully tucking her up in a fold of his cloak to keep the sharp breeze off her face.

Miellyn was limping in her thin sandals, and she shivered. I asked, "Cold?"

"No, but—I don't believe Evarin is dead, I'm afraid he got away."

For a minute the thought dimmed the luster of the morning. Then I shrugged. "He's probably buried in that big hole up there." But I knew I would never be sure.

We walked abreast, my arm around the weary, stumbling woman, and Rakhal said softly at last, "Like old times."

It wasn't old times, I knew. He would know it too, once his exultation sobered. I had outgrown my love for intrigue, and I had the feeling this was Rakhal's last adventure. It was going to take him, as he said, years to work out the equations for the transmitter. And I had a feeling my own solid, ordinary desk was going to look good to me in the morning.

But I knew now that I'd never run away from Wolf again. It was my own beloved sun that was rising. My sister was waiting for me down below, and I was bringing back her child. My best friend was walking at my side. What more could a man want?

If the memory of dark, poison-berry eyes was to haunt me in nightmares, they did not come into the waking world. I looked at Miellyn, took her slender unmanacled hand in mine, and smiled as we walked through the gates of the city. Now, after all my years on Wolf, I understood the desire to keep their women under lock and key that was its ancient custom. I vowed to myself as we went that I should waste no time finding a fetter shop and having forged therein the perfect steel chains that should bind my love's wrists to my key forever.